A WOMAN LOVED

A WOMAN LOVED

TB MARKINSON

Published by T. B. Markinson

Visit T. B. Markinson's official website at lesbianromancesbytbm.com for the latest news, book details, and other information.

Copyright © T. B. Markinson, 2018

Cover Design by Erin Dameron-Hill / EDHGraphics

Edited by Kelly Hashway

This book is copyrighted and licensed for your personal enjoyment only. All rights reserved. No part of this publication may be reproduced, stored in a retrieval system, or transmitted in any forms or by any means without the prior permission of the copyright owner. The moral rights of the author have been asserted.

This book is a work of fiction. Names, characters, businesses, places, events, and incidents are the product of the author's imagination or are used fictitiously. Any resemblance to actual persons, living or dead, events, or locales is entirely coincidental.

❀ Created with Vellum

CHAPTER ONE

I had one final task to complete the fall semester, and part of me was terrified for it to end because that meant the Petrie mad dash to Christmas would break out into full swing. For years, Christmas hardly ever merited a blip on my calendar.

That changed when I fell in love with Sarah Cavanaugh, who is now my wife and mother of our beautiful one-and-a-half-year-old twins.

Sarah adored holidays, family time, and planning.

The woman crafted to-do lists to tackle her to-do lists.

Tapping my red grading pen against the desk, I hummed along to "Little Drummer Boy," forestalling the inevitable.

The office phone rang, but I ignored it—knowing it was Sarah checking in about my ETA at home—to attend to the knock on my office door.

"Come in," I said in a forced college professor tone. Sometimes it still caught me by surprise I was a professor, in my thirties, with a wife and kids. In my formative years, I'd always believed adults understood and accepted they were fully fledged humans as well as all that entailed: mortgages, bills, insurance, wills—the list was endless. While I took care of all those things, I didn't feel so put together as a grown-up, and I was starting to suspect most of us were simply pretending to survive day to day.

Dr. Marcel's round and slightly flushed face appeared. "Still have your nose to the grindstone?"

"Ha, I'm just about to submit my grades." I waved for him to enter and take a seat, slightly embarrassed by the spartan-like feel of my office. Dr. Marcel, the dean of the history department, had an office that would make most academics drool, including a massive cherry-wood desk and leather wingback chairs. "How about you?"

He brushed his hands together. "Another semester in the books. It feels good. Although, it's weird knowing I'm retiring soon." His eyes glazed some. "Time for new blood to lead this department. I'm hoping to see you in my office one day."

Taken aback, I changed the topic. "Are you ready for Christmas?"

He chuckled. "You've met my wife. I have a feeling we're in the same boat." He leaned forward in the chair, straining his bulk. "Are you hiding?"

Dr. Marcel had known me since I was a lost and confused grad student, and sometimes it was eerie just how much he was still in tune with my inner thoughts.

I held my index finger and thumb slightly apart.

He laughed. "Take it from an old married geezer like me. It won't help." He placed his right palm on the laminated top of my desk and hoisted himself from the rickety chair. "As for me, I'm going to head home and hope she takes it easy on me. I'm not young like you. Have a very merry Christmas, Lizzie."

I stood and escorted him to the door. "You too, Dr. Marcel."

"We're looking forward to having all of you over on New Year's Day. Lydia needs her twin fix."

"The twins love any chance for extra attention."

He put his hand out for me to shake, but the glisten in his eyes made me think he would have preferred a hug. I resisted, not quite ready to challenge my personal boundaries, although having a wife and children had relaxed them. *Rome wasn't built in a day*, I reminded myself.

My personal phone rang.

I got right to it when I answered, "Submitting grades now and then I'm all yours."

"Quick question: did you ignore my call earlier?" Sarah asked in a frisky tone.

"Dr. Marcel was here," I fibbed slightly, immediately regretting it. "I mean, he was knocking on my door to wish me happy holidays. I…" My voice trailed off.

She laughed. "I had a feeling. You'll be punished later for ignoring and lying."

"Will this punishment involve naked time?"

"Depends on how quickly you get out of the office. I'm drowning here." She sounded tired but rather chipper given she loved this time of year. Why, I had no idea, and there were moments I wondered if she was on the spectrum of maniacal self-inflicted glutton for punishment. If there were such a thing.

"Give me the lowdown of what I need to do before coming home." I clicked my pen to jot down notes.

After the call, I finalized my school duties, shut down and packed my laptop, and turned off the light in my office.

* * *

MY FIRST TASK of the mad dash was to stop in Old Town, Fort Collins, at a chocolate shop Sarah was fond of. She'd provided me with a list of items to purchase for everyone's stockings. Even Maddie, our good friend, had a stocking hanging on the mantel.

Bundled up, I raised the collar on my gray wool coat to protect myself from the beginnings of a snowstorm.

On the way past a shop window, a flash of gold nabbed my attention.

I still hadn't found the perfect gift for Sarah, something I struggled with every Christmas, Valentine's, birthday, and other special occasion. Sarah was the shopper of the family, hence my detailed lists when she had to send me out into the trenches. The woman even listed the brand of milk.

Stopping in my tracks, I stared at the locket. The lights were off in the shop, and a note on the door read *By appointment only*. I made note of the number on a scrap piece of paper in my pocket and, to be on the safe side, snapped a photo with my phone.

It was well after five on December twenty-first—I was the exact opposite of my detail-oriented wife. Hopefully, I'd be able to get a hold of someone before the twenty-fourth. From the looks of the antiques in the window, the store didn't survive on walk-in traffic but rather on those interested in finding that *one* piece to complete their lives or something. How many popped in to buy an antique mahogany dining set, probably named after an English royal?

A little after seven, I walked through the garage door leading to the kitchen.

Sarah stood on the opposite side of the island, her face splattered with flour and her brow furrowed. "Did you get everything?"

"Hello to you too, beautiful." I held up the bags. "Everything on the list and some spare chocolate in case you need it. Judging by your expression, you do."

Her face softened. "I might turn you into a shopper yet."

Setting the bags on the floor near the fridge, I said, "Let's not go overboard. How are the twinkies?" I skirted the island and kissed her cheek.

"Mom and Maddie are entertaining them in the family room, hiding from me." She wiped her forehead, getting some of the flour off.

I surveyed the countertop. Mixing bowls. Flour everywhere. Egg cartons. Sugar. And other bits.

Following my eyes, she said, "I'm going to chill the dough longer than necessary for the sugar and gingerbread cookies, but I had some free time and I wanted to try to get ahead of schedule. I'm just about to start the cleanup process here."

Ahead of schedule! My inner voice was laughing her head off, which I kept to myself. I absolutely adored Sarah, even though this need of hers to plan elaborate parties confounded my practical side. But, the glint in her eyes pulled me into her orbit.

I stripped off my jacket and rolled up my shirt sleeves. "Let me do that. Why don't you make some tea or hot chocolate for everyone? Put your feet up for a bit?"

She closed one eye, appraising me. "Who are you, and what did you do with my clueless wife?"

I playacted being hurt. "Be nice, or I'll head upstairs and take a long soak in the tub. Can't feel my fingers or toes."

She boosted my hand to her mouth and kissed my fingertips. "Poor baby. Four stores and you barely survived. And it's sweater weather. Not sweater vest." She circled a finger in the air to make it perfectly clear I was crazy not to dress appropriately.

Hollering came from the family room.

Sarah sighed, closing her eyes to dig deep for her mom patience, a process I'd witnessed many times since the twins were born eighteen months ago. "Ollie's in one of her moods today. Can you bring the tea in when it's ready?" She brushed her lips against my cheek, before sashaying out of the kitchen to attend to the troublesome twin.

I filled the kettle and turned on the burner.

My eyes wandered over the mess in the kitchen. How in the hell did she get cookie dough in the crevices of the fridge door handle? Would she notice if I sent a mayday text to Miranda, our cleaner? I'd pay top dollar to have this disappear without getting my hands dirty. Sarah, though, wasn't very fond of the Petrie way—have hired help to do everything.

Fred started to cry, probably because Ollie instigated it by shoving him or something.

Maybe hiding in the kitchen wasn't the worst option at the moment.

I started stacking the dishes by the sink, rinsing them with scorching hot water and putting them in the dishwasher. How did women in the 1800s prep for the holidays? Considering that wasn't the time period I specialized in, I didn't waste too much time contemplating it. Who had time for things like that when married to the likes of Sarah?

* * *

A LITTLE AFTER TEN, I finished up dishes from dinner, and considering we had Chinese delivered, the process only involved rinsing plates and slotting them in the dishwasher, after putting away the load I'd run earlier. No one managed to fling sesame chicken on the ceiling or anything.

Sarah limped into the kitchen, looking much worse for the wear.

"Can I get you something, sweetheart?" I slung a slightly damp dish towel over my shoulder.

"Put me to bed."

"Do I need to carry you?"

"Can you?" She fell against me.

"I can try. Admittedly, I spend more time on a bicycle than lifting weights."

She laughed into my sweater vest. "Have you ever lifted weights?"

"Those are the heavy things in the gym, right?" I put my arm around her shoulders and steered us out of the kitchen to the staircase leading to all the bedrooms upstairs. "Should I draw a bath, or do you want to simply crash?"

"A bath sounds nice. You should take one. I don't think I have the energy."

I casually sniffed my armpit.

Noticing, she laughed. "I wasn't implying that; I promise. I know the end of the semester rush is hard on you, even if you took extra time avoiding coming home." I started to defend, but she plowed on. "And with all the planning for the Petrie family Christmas bash, it's a lot more than you bargained for when you put a ring on my finger." She flashed her wedding ring.

"True. Back then, I wasn't in much contact with them. Some beautiful woman encouraged me to mend broken fences, and now…"

"Who is this woman? I'd like to have a few words with her."

I'd learned it was never wise to bring up she was the cause of her own pain by insisting on going over the top for every family celebration. I veered to safer waters. "I never reveal my sources."

"Yes, you do. You footnote footnotes in your journal articles."

"Ah, well." I shrugged one shoulder. "Historians, we're sticklers for getting things right and covering our asses when others heap on attacks, which happens often since every academic is attempting to slog their way to garner prestige."

We strolled past the nursery, stopping in the doorway to gaze upon our children. "They're so cute when asleep." She rested her head on my shoulder. "And so challenging when awake. We haven't even reached the terrible twos stage." Her eyes darted toward the heavens, implying *God help us.*

She didn't budge from the doorway.

Freddie made a sound as if he was singing in his sleep.

Ollie's face was relaxed, the complete opposite of her usual awake expression.

Sarah pressed into me harder. "I know this may be the worse time to say this, considering the troubles we had with them this evening, but I really do want another baby. We aren't getting any younger, and I've always had my heart set on three. If we wait too long, I won't have the energy to chase after a toddler."

I lifted her chin with my finger and placed a soft kiss on her lips. "I know, honey. You mention it two to three times a week."

"You can be pigheaded." She kissed me sweetly.

"Pot. Kettle. Black. Let's get you in bed."

We completed the walk down the hallway.

In the bedroom, with the door mostly shut, she said, "Did your *I know* mean yes, or did it mean you know but you don't think it's a good idea?"

I perched on the foot of the bed and motioned for her to stand in front of me. "It means there isn't a thing I wouldn't do for you. I've had time to adjust to the news, and it doesn't send me into a heart-attack frenzy to contemplate it." After unzipping her jeans, I lowered them to the ground, and she stepped out of the legs. I tossed the jeans onto the chair by the window —the reading chair I'd specially purchased when we first moved in but neither of us had the energy to sit in during quiet moments.

"Do you want another baby, though?" She lifted her shirt and sweater off her head in one motion.

My eyes took in her candy-red lace bra. "Sorry, it's hard to focus at the moment."

She unclipped the bra.

I tapped the side of my forehead. "Not helping with the focusing part."

She flashed her sexy, crooked smile. "I know."

"Does this mean you don't want me to take a bath to relax?"

She straddled my lap. "It means I want an answer to my question."

I cupped her right cheek, staring into her dark eyes. "Yes, I want to have another baby. Shall we try to make a Christmas miracle?" I tapped the bed.

She yawned.

I laughed. "Bath it is."

CHAPTER TWO

December twenty-second started off with a bang.
Literally.

Sarah and I sprang out of bed and dashed to the nursery. Ollie stood in her crib, grinning. She'd managed to chuck her stuffed monkey across the room, knocking over the Diaper Genie, which had cracked open, emitting an unpleasant smell to start off the day. I attended to the problem, scrunching my nose and contemplating how such cute children could produce such noxious creations.

"Maybe being an Olympic athlete is in her future," Sarah joked, seeming much relieved that the source of the commotion was quite innocent compared to the ruckus of the crash.

"Is this the time to mention maybe it's a good thing you fell asleep before we created a Christmas miracle baby last night?" I scooped Ollie into my arms. "And how is my princess? Ready to get the day started?"

She cooed innocently in such a convincing manner, making me worry about the future.

Sarah eased Freddie into her arms, snuggling his head with her chin. "This doesn't change my mind at all."

I placed Olivia on the changing table. "Do we need to chat about making a doctor's appointment, then? Sooner rather than later?"

Sarah, at Fred's table, turned her head and goggled at me. Recovering somewhat, she asked, "Does this mean you haven't found my Christmas gift yet and this is your way around it?"

I laughed, tickling Ollie's tummy. "The women in this family! Going to make me gray before my time."

I sensed Sarah's eye roll. "What about you, Freddie?" She wiggled his feet. "Would you like a baby brother?"

"I'm not sure you can order up a baby boy like that." I fastened Ollie's fresh diaper. "Need I remind you we were aiming for only one last time?"

"Oh, no. You've said that before, *dear*," she said with her special emphasis. "Help me set up the twins for breakfast, and then you can hop in the shower and wash off the rude awakening. I need to send you out for a few last-minute items."

"Nothing would make me happier than to leave the comfort of our warm home and head out into the frenzied days before Christmas Eve. Should we crack the window to air it out some?"

"Yes to the window and I know how much you love to shop any time of the year. This is my way of giving in to all your desires." She batted her eyelashes.

"Since you love lists, I can compile one that includes my actual desires. And shopping will never be on it."

We both held a child in our arms, staring into each other's eyes.

"No need. I can always see what you're craving."

* * *

THE DOOR to the shop was locked. I yanked my phone out of my jeans pocket to consult the time. I was five minutes early.

I blew into my hands, cursing my aversion to gloves.

An older gentleman who looked like he just stepped out of an English pub, circa 1940, approached from my left, making his way from town center. "Mrs. Petrie?"

"Lizzie, please."

He tilted his head, gripping his cane with both hands. "How can I help you today?"

I'd explained to the woman on the phone I wanted to purchase the locket in the window, but apparently, this man didn't get that part of my message.

I pointed to it in the window. "I'd like to buy that for my—" I stopped myself from saying wife to the crumpled old man, who may or may not approve of same-sex couples. It was hit or miss in Colorado. Two-hours away resided the headquarters for Focus on the Family, an active opponent of homosexuality, who believed in conversion therapies. "Mom," I said, disappointed in myself but not wanting to waste the energy.

"A beautiful piece. Let's go in." It took him a few stabs to get the key into the lock. Holding the door for me, making me feel awkward since I should be holding it for him, he waved me inside.

The inside smelled like a grandparents' basement, or so I assumed. "You have some lovely things here," I said, trying not to breathe in too deeply.

He nodded appreciatively.

I sat in the chair next to his desk, after he made a bossy gesture for me to take a seat, which I interpreted to mean he didn't want me wandering around the store, browsing. He had no worries there. If Maddie were with me, she wouldn't be able to contain herself.

After gathering the locket, he sat in his chair. "This is quite the piece." He held it in his wrinkled and liver-spotted hand. "Twelve carat gold fill. Ruby Victorian paste stone and seed pearls. This locket was made in Providence, somewhere between 1880 and 1920." He flipped it open. "Do you have a sibling?"

"Yes," I said, perplexed.

"You can slip in both photos for your mother."

I nodded. "That's the plan." Albeit, it would be photos of Freddie and Ollie.

He turned it over. "On the back are the initials O, F, and C."

I leaned closer. "Really?" We had discussed potential names for our third child, and the letter C was perfect for the names under consideration.

Maybe he sensed my keenness, because his sharp smile reminded me of a used car salesman dealing with a live one.

Nice job, Lizzie.

He got to his feet, his knees cracking. "I have a twenty-four-inch gold chain that would pair nicely with this." He disappeared into the back of the shop.

I pulled my wallet out of my messenger bag.

"Here it is." He held it between a thumb and forefinger.

"Perfect. How much do I owe you?"

He retook his seat. "Would nineteen hundred suit you?"

"Do you prefer credit or check?"

* * *

BY THE TIME I finished at the grocery store, it was after eleven, so I phoned Maddie. She was taking time off from her design business for the rest of the year.

"It's still kinda early, you know." Her voice was overly peppy, clueing me in her complaint was intended to be playful.

"Do you have a recent photo of the twins together?" I'd need to save a space in the locket for the Christmas miracle.

"Not the question I was expecting, but yes. I have quite a few. Do you want to come over so we can chat?"

For the past year, Maddie had been an avid photographer, purely a hobby, and the twins were one of her favorite subjects.

"Sounds great. I'm finalizing some things for Sarah. Up next on my shopping list is"—I consulted the paper and read with uncertainty in my voice—"Hobby Lobby."

"She must be desperate or insane to send you there."

I groaned. "What does she really need from there? Can't I go to Jorie's shop instead? She'd take pity on me." I scanned Sarah's shopping items.

"Jorie works in a toy store. Hobby Lobby is an arts and crafts store."

"So, that's a no, then?"

"Hard no. Totally different things. Besides, Jorie's out of town for the holiday. Don't worry. I'm around the corner and will pop in to help. We can't have you wandering the aisles for hours never to be seen again. That'd ruin Sarah's holiday."

* * *

THAT NIGHT, I sat at the kitchen table as Sarah demonstrated how to assemble the placeholders she wanted me to make for Christmas Eve dinner.

Her latest brainstorm was to create one new homemade article each season so that in twenty years we'd have a lot of junk. I kept the last thought to myself, naturally.

"Glue the bottom of the pinecone, and stick it on the gold painted Styrofoam square, like this." She used the glue gun. "Cut the extra-long wooden toothpick so it's this long." She held it up, and it looked to be roughly eight inches. "Glue a wood ball on top of the pinecone, with the hole facing up. Fill the hole with glue, and stick the toothpick into the glue." Again, she used the gun. "Cut the red felt into a triangle and this shape." She held up a cutout that was chunky at the top and narrow at the bottoms. "Glue one of the corners of the triangle, and attach the other corner to make a hat." She shredded one of the cotton balls. "Use this to fill the hat, and then place it over the toothpick onto the head. Glue the hat down. Take this piece of fabric and wrap it around the neck for the scarf." With one eye squinted, Sarah judged if I was still with her, and I nodded. "Hang the tiny bell on this gold chain, and put it around the neck." She smiled as her creation started taking shape. "Glue a small cotton ball on top of the red hat." She picked up a black marker. "Draw two eyeballs and a mouth. And voilà!" She held up her pinecone man. "Do you think you can manage the rest? Maddie and I are going to tackle the gingerbread house."

"You won't be far in case I need you?" I eyed the supplies, trying to remember all the steps.

"Sometimes, you're adorable, and I forget you have a PhD." She patted my cheek.

"That didn't answer my question," I muttered under my breath.

My first task was to brew a cup of strong black tea.

That mission accomplished, I set out to make an assembly line of sorts, cutting all the red felt first into thirteen hats and scarves. Next, I snipped all the toothpicks. By the time I prepped everything, I dove in with my first attempt.

When I completed it, I compared it to Sarah's man. Mine had a childish quality. Was that her goal and the reason she'd tasked me with this? To tell people years from now the twins made them, not me?

On the third creation, Maddie entered the kitchen. "I'm going to make some eggnog. You want some?"

"Not sure that would mesh well with operating a hot glue gun."

"Come on. Live a little, and stop acting like an old lady." She surveyed my progress. "I have to admit, when I showed Sarah the YouTube clip for this"—she waved to the supplies—"I didn't know she'd go through with it and force you to make these."

"You have met my wife, right? Raising twins hasn't slowed down her mania for celebrations."

Maddie tilted her head back, laughing. "You should see the gingerbread house operation in the dining room. You have it easy; trust me." She made a *pshaw* sound, getting to work on the eggnog, bobbing her head to the Christmas tunes Sarah had playing on the recently installed speakers throughout the bottom floor of the house.

The twins were in their room, safe in their beds. I glanced at the monitors on my left, smiling.

Maddie set down a cup for me. "For when you finish." She sat on the chair next to me, sipping her drink. "I hear you've finally given in."

I prepped a cotton ball for one of the hats. "About what?" I peeked to ensure Sarah wasn't within earshot. "Not sure you noticed, but I give in to Sarah a lot." I squirted some glue, but the gun slipped in my hand, making contact with one of my fingers holding the cotton ball in place. "Fuck! That's hot!" I shook my finger.

Maddie reached out. "Let me see."

The tiny globule of glue continued to burn.

"It needs to harden so we can get it off." Maddie blew onto it.

"What's wrong?" Sarah approached with a mother-hen look.

"Lizzie's showing off her exceptional craft skills." Maddie scraped the glue, but it wasn't relenting quite yet.

Sarah planted a kiss on top of my head. "Where are the green guys?"

I cranked my neck to stare up into her eyes. "What green guys?"

"There's green felt in addition to red." She pointed at the fabric.

I hadn't noticed the pile of green felt at all, and I had zero recollection of buying it. I nodded. "Oh, yeah. I was getting to them."

Maddie, with narrowed eyes, started to say something but then went back to attending to my finger. "I think you'll live."

Sarah kissed the top of my head again. "Okay, Maddie, we have some work to do. Chop-chop." She slapped her hands together.

They marched out, Maddie glancing at me over her shoulder as if I could rescue her.

I pointed to the green felt and shrugged.

* * *

SARAH AND MADDIE were still toiling with their project, while I sat on one of the couches in the library, hiding. If either of them asked, I'd claim I was reading a book to prep for the spring semester. To give credence to my cover story, I had a book about the origins of the Hitler Youth open in my lap, with pen and notepad at the ready. This break, I did plan on prepping for the upcoming semester, but what I really wanted was to carve out time to work on a historical novel I'd started many months ago, which had to be set aside for the remaining few weeks of the semester. At the moment, feigning writing seemed like too much work, so I stuck with the Hitler Youth ruse.

The door opened, and I snapped to attention, jotting down the words *Hitler Youth*. Given the title of the book and my expertise on the subject, it wasn't all that convincing, but my brain was too muddled to outsmart Sarah.

Sarah, with glass in hand, sat on the couch next to me. "Is it next year yet?"

"Getting closer every minute." I brushed some hair off her cheek.

"Why do you insist on these elaborate plans every holiday?"

She fell back onto the couch with a scooch too much flair. "I'm not as young as I used to be, you know."

Ignoring her sarcasm since she was the one who insisted on these parties, I said, "Clearly, I'm a sociopath."

She nodded, snuggling against me. "Good thing you're cute."

I rested my head on hers. "Good thing you're sexy as hell."

"I may have overshot a bit this year."

Knowing it was best to take this as a silent victory, I said, "We're almost over the finish line. Are you ready for me to pour you into bed?"

"Can we stay here a little longer? You can keep pretending to read." She nudged my side with her elbow.

"Honestly, I can't get away with anything."

She yawned into my sweater. "Next time, try having the book right side up."

"What?" I looked, and it was right side up.

"Gotcha, but I had a feeling. You never drink alcohol when trying to get actual work done."

"That's what gave me away? I thought the notebook would be a nice touch." I set the notebook and pen down on the end table.

"I do give you credit for that, but I'm not sure I should condone this type of behavior."

Time for a diversion, Lizzie style. "Did Maddie go home, or is she in the guest bedroom?"

"Bedroom. I'm hoping she'll be kind enough to get the kiddos up in the morning like she does sometimes."

"They do love their aunt." It was my turn to yawn.

"I'm calling it. Let's put this day in the books and get some sleep. Who knows how Ollie will wake us tomorrow morning?"

In our bedroom, after stripping off our clothes, we both opted to sleep in the nude. Something Sarah had almost always done pre-twinkies.

Under the covers, Sarah rested her chin on my chest, her eyes a sexy pool of rich chocolate.

Something down below stirred.

Maybe she sensed it, because she moved to kiss me.

Softly.

Sweetly.

I wanted more.

So, I deepened it.

All tiredness seeped from my bones, and red-hot passion surged through me.

I rolled Sarah onto her back, shoving my hip between her legs.

She welcomed it by ramping up the heat of the kiss.

My hip gyrated into her.

My hand trailed down her side.

Sometimes it still amazed me how much I craved Sarah. After all these years. The silly spats. The complications. The happy times. Having twins. The days we stumbled into bed, exhausted. No matter what, my love for Sarah compounded daily. And my desire increased tenfold. I couldn't imagine not being able to touch her. Hold her. Kiss her. Be inside her.

And every time was like falling in love all over again.

She held my face in both hands as I hovered over her, staring into her gorgeous eyes. "What?"

"You're amazing, Sarah. The way you make me feel. I wish I could marry you again and again and again."

Her eyes misted, but she managed to joke, "Says the woman who went into a tailspin when I wanted to settle down."

"Says the woman who knew exactly what I wanted, even if I was a fucking moron."

She smiled, not speaking yet, telling me with her eyes she did and would love and protect me until my dying day. I would do the same for her.

I kissed away her tears, landing on her mouth for the sweetest kiss.

My hip still moved into her below, tenderly and slowly.

Our desire had switched gears from fucking to making love.

I left a trail of kisses, from her lips, down her chin, into the dip of her throat, to her right breast. Where I lingered, blissfully bringing her nipple to life with my tongue, grazing it slightly with my teeth. Working my way across her chest, savoring the taste of her skin, I landed on her other nipple, which met me with eager anticipation.

Sarah let out a tiny gasp.

My hip dug into her harder.

She gasped again.

I made my move to head further south, knowing her breasts would always be there for my next visit.

As I traveled down her ticklish and sensitive side, Sarah writhed, reaching overhead, fisting the pillow with both hands. Her back arched slightly, giving me access to her stomach and allowing my fingers to reach under her, holding her up.

I would always hold her up.

No matter how hard things got.

Nothing would stop me from loving her.

My tongue dipped into her belly button, cutting downward to where I belonged.

Over her coarse hair, loving how it scraped against my chin, as if embedding the moment into my skin. My soul. My heart.

Sarah's musky scent beckoned.

I inhaled deeply.

Again.

She was really squirming now.

Sarah wanted me.

My tongue separated her wet lips.

Dear God, how had this lovely creature walked on the same Earth for over twenty years before I met her?

Every time we made love, it was evident we were always meant to find each other.

To love each other.

To be there forever.

I tasted her from inside, as deep as my tongue allowed.

A spurt escaped from me, and I moaned into Sarah.

Her body welcomed it.

My tongue slid upward.

Sarah's body hitched in anticipation.

I diverted to her inner thigh.

Sarah's groan was momentarily displeased—or should I say overly suggestive?

"Patience," I mumbled into her flesh.

"Paybacks are hell."

"I'll hold you to that." Between her legs, I had the best view on the planet.

She couldn't resist a sexy laugh.

I eased two fingers inside her, my eyes devouring the effect this had on her.

Pushing in harder.

Deeper still.

Moving my mouth closer to where she wanted me.

And then I was home.

I flicked her clit with my tongue. Once. Twice. Three times.

Shoving harder inside.

Taking her in my mouth.

Sarah's hands were on my head, pulling me into her. It took effort to stay where she needed me, but I wouldn't let her down. Not ever. Together, we reached the next stage of making love. Where the expectations were high. As much as the emotions. Only two people who adored each other could make love as if they'd die if they couldn't.

"Oh, Lizzie," she moaned, adding, "I love you."

It always amazed me how in tune she was with me at all times.

She reached bliss, making me the happiest person on the planet.

The way it should always be.

* * *

BOTH OF US SPENT, I lay in her arms.

"I love the things you do to me," she whispered.

My fingers walked over her breast. "I need to get my fill of these before you get pregnant again."

"Maybe they won't be so sore this time around," she said without much conviction.

"Just in case, be prepared for regular breast fondling until we officially test the theory."

"I think that's something I can adjust to, if forced upon me." She squeezed me tightly. "You sure you don't want to carry the baby this time?" Her eyes teased.

"And deny you the pleasure? Don't you remember how much you loved it? And, it'll save you from having your eggs sucked out since you want to use yours this time." I shivered still remembering that experience.

"Yeah, that's why. One day of pain over being pregnant nine months, not to mention delivery."

"Hey now, if I remember correctly—"

She smothered my mouth with her hand. "I know. Everything was my idea." She yawned. "It's so late. Why aren't we falling asleep?"

"Life is so cruel, making us love each other."

"Should I speak to God about this?"

"Please don't. While I'll be a fucking zombie tomorrow, I won't mind one bit."

"We do have a full day." Her voice was teasing. Or was she spurring me for more?

"Are you saying we should close our eyes?"

"You can keep your eyes closed if you want. That won't stop me."

I was on my back in a heartbeat, with Sarah on top.

CHAPTER THREE

"You look like shit," Maddie greeted me in the kitchen.

"Such a sweet talker." I kissed Sarah's cheek on my way to fill the teakettle for a much-needed cup of English breakfast tea as strong as I could make it to power through another day of Christmas prep.

Sarah stood at the counter, with pen and clipboard in hand. "Okay, Maddie, you're in charge of rolling out the cookie dough." She plopped the gallon-sized Ziplock bag of cookie cutters on the granite countertop.

The twins wandered the kitchen on their chubby legs, Freddie with a glob of oatmeal in his hair. "Come here, little man." I leaned down with a wet washcloth. "Did Aunt Maddie feed you this morning?"

"Someone had to take care of your children," she defended.

"For which I'll always be grateful, and should I remind you that you're their honorary aunt? Did you not read the fine print?" I gave Fred a hug, and he set off to the front room, tailing Sarah.

Maddie eyed the back of Sarah and her two ducklings, who

were hot on her heels. "What gives? I got tasked with baking, and she didn't bark any orders at you."

"My secret powers." I waggled my fingers magician-like.

"Yuck. You two had sex while I was staying the night!"

With a hand on my heart, I said, "Would we do that?"

"It's sickening, sometimes, how much you two love each other."

"Not sure I can change that to suit your needs."

"But it can't be just that. Have you noticed how she's been preoccupied? More than normal?"

I hadn't, really. Part of me suspected Maddie was fishing. For what, though?

Sarah popped her head around the door. "Sweetheart, can I borrow you for a second? The angel on the tree is off-kilter."

As I marched by Maddie, she muttered, "I may have to sleep with her to get better treatment."

I shot her a nasty look.

Maddie laughed.

In the living room, Sarah asked, "What was that about?"

"Just Maddie being Maddie." I eyed the tree, confused.

Sarah threaded her arms around my neck. "I wanted a proper good morning kiss, minus Maddie."

"My pleasure, and if you don't mind, can you add one of these kisses every hour on the hour for the rest of the year?"

"Just this year?"

"Forever, then."

We locked lips.

Longer than usual at this time of day.

Not that I was complaining.

Pulling apart, Sarah still held on, resting her head on my shoulder.

Freddie cooed, circling one of the ottomans in the room.

Olivia howled.

We both turned our attention to our daughter.

"She's been hanging out with Aunt Maddie too much," I said before going to Ollie. "How about you help me make some toast?" I scooped her up onto my hip. "Are you hungry?" I asked Sarah.

She shook her head, already lost in her next task.

* * *

GABE AND ALLEN arrived around eleven.

Maddie had set up the kitchen table as Christmas cookie decorating central. White, blue, red, and green frosting. Sprinkles. Red hots. Three decorating bags with fine tips. Chocolate kisses. Small nonpareils. Crushed candy canes.

Allen, my half brother, poked his finger at one of the bowls. "What are those?"

Maddie answered, "Edible silver leaf."

Allen placed one on his tongue.

"They're for the cookies, Al." Gabe, my stepbrother, placed a hand on Allen's shoulder. "I'll leave you guys to this. I hear there's a manly task for me." He beat his chest like Tarzan.

Allen started to balk, but Maddie and I silenced him.

When Gabe left the kitchen, Maddie whispered, "You're safer and warmer with us."

"What's Sarah going to do to him?" His voice was aghast, making it clear that even my youngest sibling had grown accustomed to Sarah's party ways.

"Do you remember the first time you came over for Christmas and the backyard was lit up with lights?" When he nodded, I said, "Sarah has quadrupled the amount, but we haven't had time to set everything up. Gabe will be lucky to finish by midnight. And fingers crossed Sarah's plan doesn't plunge the entire Front Range into a blackout. Can I be sued?"

"You had the electrician out?" Maddie asked, her brow creased.

"Yep. Let's not talk about the bill." I mimed we should never discuss the topic again.

"You really are pussy-whipped, you know that?"

Allen nodded his agreement with Maddie's assessment.

"Please, you aren't telling me anything I don't know. Speaking of, we need to get cracking on these." I waved to the supplies and then said behind the back of my hand, "Sarah has a whip and isn't afraid to use it."

"I need hot chocolate first. It's illegal to decorate Christmas cookies without it. You two?" Maddie looked to me and then Allen.

"I don't want to break any laws." Allen smiled, taking a seat at the table, selecting a sugar cookie in the shape of a reindeer to frost.

While both Allen and Gabe enjoyed guy-like pursuits, such as college football, they were both comfortable doing purported feminine tasks. Gabe managed one of his mom's flower shops. Allen liked decorating cookies and had mentioned recently wanting to learn how to bake after watching an episode of *The Great British Bake Off*. Both comfortably floated between the two spheres as if they didn't exist, and I suspected that was Helen's doing. It made me appreciate Sarah's insistence our children be themselves at all times. I wondered how Peter and I would have turned out if we had loving and supportive parents.

Moments later, after each of us had a steaming mug of chocolatey goodness, Sarah marched Gabe outside, with her hand-drawn schematic of the Christmas light display. Gabe looked longingly at the cookie table. Allen waved to his sibling, while taking a sip, the marshmallow smearing his upper lip.

Maddie and I laughed, sounding like maniacal holiday helpers.

Rose arrived thirty or so minutes later, surveying the kitchen, and then peeked outside at Gabe on a ladder. She fished her phone out of her bag. "Troy, I think Gabe needs your help. I know what Sarah said, but she's… Just come over, please."

"I think they need the National Guard." Maddie speckled a Santa Claus with three white dots.

"She's lost her mind this year." Rose stood at the breakfast nook window. "Shush, she's coming inside."

The kitchen door leading to the back deck opened. Sarah stomped the three-day-old snow off her boots. "Mom, just the person I wanted."

Rose's pupils tripled in size.

Part of me felt bad for her.

But Rose was on her own.

Helen trooped into the kitchen, holding a silver oval basket containing white lilies, red carnations, some peppy white flowers I didn't know the name of, holly with berries, and gold glitter balls. "Allen, honey, can you help me get the rest of the arrangements out of the truck."

"Truck?" I asked.

Helen rolled her eyes. "It's best if you stay in here, or your mind will be blown, Lizzie." With both hands, she mimicked my head exploding.

Moments later, Allen stalked by with a red cylinder vase with holly and berries, evergreens, white roses, and lilies with red middles.

"That one goes on the coffee table in the family room," instructed Sarah, extending her finger.

Flashes of color snagged my attention every so often as Maddie and I avoided Madame Taskmaster's eyes every time she came into view.

Troy walked by with his head hanging down on his way to the backyard as if marching to his doom.

Gabe came in briefly for a cup of coffee, standing at the kitchen sink window, quietly eying his work or possibly the amount he had left. I gave him an *attaboy* smile. He stared blankly and resignedly went back out into the cold.

"It's possible my wife broke your boyfriend," I whispered.

"Yesterday, he was so excited about this project. I didn't have the heart to warn him," Maddie whispered behind a Frosty cookie she was smearing with pink icing.

"Probably for the best. I'll do my best to time our next child close to December twenty-fifth so she won't have the energy for all this."

Maddie's expression brightened. "All of us would be ever so grateful."

I laughed. "A Christmas miracle to preemptively save Sarah from breaking all of our holiday spirit in the years to come."

Maddie grinned, but it clouded over. "She may have thought of that and has already begun her planning."

My heart stilled, and I sucked in a deep breath. "Surely not. How can she manage this?" I waved to everything going on around us: cookies, flowers, lights, and everything I couldn't see from my vantage point. "And another one at the same time. It's a challenge for her to up her game every time, but double planning at once—I can't fathom that."

"I know," she said with grave concern in her voice. "We may have to hold an intervention or commit her."

Rose walked by, her cheeks flushed.

A cry from one of the monitors compelled me to a standing position. "Naptime is over. You got this?"

Maddie shrugged.

* * *

GABE AND TROY trooped inside around eight at night, laughing and smacking each other on the shoulders as if returning from a grueling battle, relieved to have survived.

"Ladies and Allen," Gabe started, tossing his brother a

ribbing look only brothers can share. "The Christmas magic awaits you outside."

Sarah and I bundled up the twins in their winter jackets and then shrugged into ours.

"Before I flip on the switch to officially start Christmas, I think we need to applaud the woman behind everything. We may not appreciate her directions all the time"—Gabe winked at Sarah—"but she's a true artist." Gabe waggled one foot of each twin. "Your mommy loves you two this much." He switched on the lights.

"My eyes." Maddie flung an arm over her face.

Freddie, on Sarah's hip, reached out with both hands as if trying to touch the lights, giggling.

In my arms, Ollie was completely silent, for once, her eyes wide with a big smile on her face.

Troy wrapped an arm around Rose's shoulders, and she rested her head against him.

My gaze swept over the massive Frosty tucked into the corner of the yard. There was a nativity scene. Elves in a toy shop. More Frostys spread out. Snoopy on his doghouse, which had lights. Santas in every possible pose. Rudolphs. Giant gold bells. Wrapped gifts. White lights were wrapped around the trunks and lower branches of the three oak trees. Colorful lights hung in the branches of the Aspens.

Gabe wrapped an arm around Maddie. "What do you think?" He puffed out his chest.

"Took you two long enough."

The air in his chest deflated some.

It started to snow, the lights reflecting on the water droplets when they made contact on top of the twins' hoods.

The neighbor next to us flipped on their back patio light, which was useless considering astronauts orbiting Earth could probably see the display.

"Perhaps we can kill the lights until Christmas Eve," I suggested.

Much to my surprise, Sarah readily agreed and headed inside with her mom, chatting about God knows what.

Gabe and Troy watched everyone else retreat inside.

I held Ollie closer to keep her warm. "I know it's hard. All this work for a fleeting victorious feeling."

Gabe nodded as if stunned.

Troy switched off the lights.

"Can I buy you two a whiskey by the fire?" I asked.

"That would be nice." Gabe took Ollie in his arms. "I need a hug, baby girl."

Olivia happily obliged.

* * *

I PUT the twinkies down for the night and stayed in the nursery, rocking in the chair, watching them fall asleep.

Sarah joined me, speaking in the hushed voice we'd both mastered. "They're completely zonked out."

I placed my arm through her legs, hugging her left thigh. "It's my favorite time of night. Seeing them drift into dreamworld."

"You going to stay in here for a bit?" she asked. "Maddie's making mulled wine."

"Sounds dangerous, especially knowing Maddie is in charge. You sure that's wise?"

"You know me. I like to live on the edge."

"Do you have a to-do list for that?" I whispered.

She bumped her hip into the chair. "Everyone is making it clear I went slightly overboard this year. Earlier, when Gabe plugged in the lights... the planning didn't seem that involved, but the lights..." Her voice trailed off.

I pulled her into my lap. "Ollie was impressed. So was Fred."

"They are who I do it for."

"I know, and I think everyone understands. You might want to work on your *barking orders* style, though. Like bring it down a notch or ten."

She leaned into me. "I just want everything to be perfect. There have been so many changes in our family lately and… I don't know."

"You feel pressure to hold everything and everyone together," I stated instead of asking, brushing my cheek against hers.

"Yes. I think you hit the nail on the head on that one."

"Not everything is on your shoulders. Let some of us help carry the burden." I kissed the side of her head.

"Now you tell me, after everything is almost said and done."

"Timing is my specialty."

"I'm going downstairs to make sure Maddie doesn't burn the place down."

I laughed quietly. "You can't stop the need to control, can you? And, how does one burn down a house while making mulled wine? I'm no whiz in the kitchen, but—"

"Please, we're talking about Maddie. She can cause major destruction watering a plant just for shits and giggles." She kissed me on the lips to shut me up, not that I was complaining, and then rose. "Don't hide too long."

"A few more minutes. I feel like I missed so much time with them during the semester."

Sarah stared at me with a funny look on her face. "You never cease to amaze me."

"When you start at the bottom,"—I held my hand to indicate subbasement level—"it's easy to impress."

She pressed her cheek against the doorjamb. "Was that your plan from the start?"

"You're the planner, dear. I'm more the type who was treading water."

Her eyes darted upward. "Tell me about it."

After she left, I could hear the twins breathing, soothing my mind from all the fears rampaging my thoughts since Sarah and I had agreed to get pregnant again. Freddie's birth hadn't been easy. He hadn't breathed on his own for the most terrifying seconds of my life. And the thought of anything happening to Sarah...

I sucked in a deep breath.

Moonlight trickled into the window, and I could see the North Star. I made a silent wish for a safe pregnancy and birth if Sarah became pregnant again.

Standing, I went to Fred's bed, kissed my fingertips, and pressed it to his forehead before repeating the action for Ollie. "Sweet dreams, you two."

Downstairs, I found Gabe, Maddie, and Sarah in the library, laughing.

Sarah beamed at me. "I missed you." Her cheeks were flushed, her eyes glossy from the booze. But I knew she meant it.

"Me too."

Maddie got to her feet. "I'll get you a glass of deliciousness."

"I'll take another." Sarah thrust hers in Maddie's direction.

I took a seat on the couch next to Sarah. "Did I miss anything?"

"We were sharing Christmas memories," Sarah said. "Poor Gabe didn't get a guitar when he was seven, and he's never recovered."

He rubbed his chin. "I could have been a rock star."

"Yeah, that's the reason," Sarah deadpanned, adding, "I've heard you sing."

He didn't miss a beat. "So, you know I had potential."

"Oh, the male ego is truly endless." She sneered.

"I don't know what you mean."

"You wouldn't. That's the problem." Sarah smacked her own leg, hard.

He showed his palms and them moved them back as if miming walking away. "What about you, Lizzie? What gift did you want from Santa but never got?"

I cocked my head in Sarah's direction. "I... I really don't know. Christmas wasn't really a big deal. Not for Peter and me. Mom went all out entertaining Dad's business clients. Those Christmas day brunches are what I remember most. Not gifts." I paused. "Was the holiday a big deal in your home?" I asked Gabe in a quiet voice.

"Oh yes. We celebrated on Christmas Eve, and Mom and Char—" He stopped as if slugged in the chest. "I... I should help Maddie." He rose and fled.

"You okay?" Sarah asked.

I nodded. "It's weird. Most of the time I'm able to divorce the knowledge that my father had a separate family. Sometimes, though..." I hitched a shoulder. "I shouldn't have asked. That wasn't fair to Gabe. Morbid curiosity, I guess."

"It wasn't unfair to ask, really. In the grand scheme of things, you two have only known each other for a short time. Naturally, both of you are curious about the other." Sarah stretched her arms overhead. "Do you notice how he never mentions his father? And I'm curious what his relationship with his mother is really like. At one point, he had her all to himself, and then Charles entered the picture. Gabe adores Allen, but it would be hard, not having his father around and seeing Allen with his mom and Charles. Did he ever feel pushed out? I think you and Gabe have more in common than you think. Not just golf," she attempted to suppress a smile since golf was a new thing she encouraged as a way for me to spend more time with my siblings, new and old, and so far, my skills were subpar.

"Probably." That was too much to ponder at the moment. "What gift did young Sarah want that she never got?"

"Is it awful of me to say I got everything I wanted."

"If true, no. That's the way it should be. And knowing you had everything you wanted warms my heart. What about now? What do you want?"

"I have everything I want or could possibly need. Stop trying to buy me the perfect gift. I don't need it."

"Shall I return it, then?"

Her face flushed. "And ruin the effort you put into finding it?"

"That's what I thought. And I'm looking forward to seeing what you got me."

She placed a hand over her mouth. "I knew I was forgetting something!"

"Hardy har har."

She kept up the act. Or at least I think she was acting. Would it be possible for her to drop the Lizzie ball?

Gabe and Maddie crashed back into the room, each carrying two mugs of mulled wine.

"Salvation is here!" Maddie held up her hands. "You'll thank me, Lizzie. Nothing in life can be bad when drinking my special mulled wine brew."

CHAPTER FOUR

I rolled over in bed, groaning.

Sarah matched my displeasure with her own growl. "What time is it?"

I squinted at the clock, the red light fuzzier than usual. "Not sure you really want to know."

"What happened?" She snuggled into my arms.

"Maddie's mulled wine—the devil's brew." I kissed her head. "Merry almost Christmas."

"There's nothing merry about today." She rolled over, reaching for her phone. After several seconds, she said, "Mom, I'll pay you a thousand dollars to come get the twins." There was a pause. "No, I'm not sick. Just…" Another pause. "Thanks."

"There are perks to having one's mother-in-law around the corner." I opened one eye to judge Sarah's mood. "Do you think you can get some more rest?"

"Water first."

I got up and stumbled into the master bathroom to fill up two water glasses.

Sarah gulped hers, wrapped her hands around her head, and rolled over.

Two hours later, I made my way to the kitchen to make coffee for Sarah and tea for me.

Maddie sat on the barstool, coffee cup in hand, reading the screen on her iPhone. "Whose brilliant idea was it to invite your entire family for Christmas Eve dinner? When hungover?"

"I thought your mulled wine was our salvation," I mocked.

"We have T-minus nine hours before everyone is expected. And you know the Petries. Never late."

"It's true. When I had 8:00 a.m. classes in college, I had my butt in the seat every day exactly at 7:53."

"Why fifty-three? Why not 7:55?"

I shrugged. "Not sure really. Do we really want to psychoanalyze me today of all days? I'm going to make more coffee for Sarah. Do you need a refill?"

She nodded.

"What about Gabe? Is he still asleep in the guest bedroom?"

"I think I'm going to claim the room. I spend more time here or at Gabe's than at home. A complete waste of rent." She sipped her drink. "And, no, Gabe rolled out of bed at six for work. He's still in his twenties. I think he muttered something about Christmas orders or along those lines." She waved a hand implying she hadn't been listening or didn't care. "Do you think it wise to wake Sarah yet? Rose and Troy have the twinks."

I placed my palms on the countertop. "It's a catch-22, really. She's been going nonstop and, thanks to you, has a hangover from hell. But if I let her sleep, she'll panic about her to-do list." I waggled my hands in the air, determining which was the lesser of two evils. "What do you think?"

"You're asking me for advice?" She clutched the front of her long-sleeve. "Look at you, growing as an adult."

I rolled my eyes.

She laughed. "It's a catch-22 for us as well. We can relax a bit longer or be under the control of Madame Taskmaster."

"I know, but I sleep in the same bed as Madame Taskmaster. And… she scares me sometimes." Not to mention I enjoyed having sex with her, and pissing her off was one of the best ways to cut me off for the foreseeable future.

"Afraid she'll smother you with a pillow?"

"Something like that. Besides, all of this is partly my fault. She has difficult in-laws, and she's doing everything she can to help me navigate the Petrie quicksand and make things as normal as possible for our children."

"Gabe feels terrible, by the way."

"Maybe you shouldn't be in charge of alcohol." I filled the coffee pot, aware my only option was to rouse Sarah from her hungover slumber—or suffer the taskmaster's consequences. I'd rather suffer than Sarah. In any situation.

"Not about that. He'd had too much to drink when you asked him about Christmas with his mom and Charles."

I turned the burner on to heat up the teakettle. With my back to her, I said, "I shouldn't have asked. It's just odd, sometimes, knowing my father was more of a father to him than to me. And Peter, really."

"I don't think that's true. About you not asking. You have the right to know. Besides, Gabe really likes you, Lizzie. Looks up to you, actually. Your drive to succeed. He's even more determined to turn his mom's shops into the only online store for flowers and gardening." Her voice was soft, lacking her usual snark. "You two should hang out more, just the two of you. Talk. About feelings and such. You know the stuff you hate, and admittedly, Gabe isn't that great at it either, but it'll help you two get to know each other better."

I wheeled about. "Why does growing as an adult involve so much talking? It's my least favorite activity right after cleaning the toilet."

Her smile confirmed she understood how much she was asking of me, but she wouldn't give up. I didn't think she meant to push me today, though.

A creak on the stairs drew our attention.

Maddie and I locked eyes momentarily before chuckling.

"And so it begins," she whispered.

Still in pajamas and a floral robe, Sarah entered, yawning and bleary-eyed. "Coffee, stat."

"Almost ready. I was going to bring it up to you."

She plopped onto the barstool next to Maddie. "What'd I miss?"

"Christmas. The twins loved it. The Petries behaved. Dinner was a smashing success." Maddie made checkmarks in the air after every fib.

Sarah narrowed her eyes. "You know, I wish everything you said was true."

The coffee pot gurgled. I poured the black liquid into Sarah's *I haven't had my coffee yet; don't make me kill you* mug, a gift from Maddie. "Sugar this morning?"

She grunted, "Yes."

That was a bad sign.

Then she said, "Two scoops."

Doubly bad sign.

"Of course, sweetheart. Are you hungry? I can whip up some pancakes."

"Please," Maddie answered, and I was certain she answered for Sarah, who, more than likely, would have refused in order to get the to-do list going.

I didn't know how to tell her we could have all the food catered and hire party planners to save her from the trouble. For Sarah, the effort was her way of loving her family.

Sarah flicked her fingers, indicating whatever.

"While I make breakfast, why don't you take a long, hot shower?"

Sarah scooped up her cup and left.

"Quick thinking about the pancakes and shower," Maddie said.

"Glad you think so, because you have to make the pancakes. We all know I can't cook." I pitched my hands in the air, demonstrating I was useless in the kitchen.

"I didn't see that coming. Nicely played. But you aren't escaping to the library. You can help me gather everything. First, another cup please." She banged her cup on the counter.

CHAPTER FIVE

Sarah shoved her breakfast plate away. "Okay, you two, get cracking on wrapping the remaining gifts. Lizzie, you tackle the twins' presents and let Maddie do the rest." Sarah jerked her thumb over her shoulder to a pile of boxes, wrapping paper, ribbons, and bows sitting on the twins' craft table tucked into the corner of the family room.

"Yeah, the twins won't notice if the images don't align, the bow is off center, and the ribbon's in tatters—you aren't the most meticulous wrapper. Just saying." Maddie's smart-ass smile didn't rile me.

"Totally okay with that. Let's get cracking. My part should be done in twenty." I tapped the face of my sports watch.

"Right after I prep much-needed Bloody Marys." Maddie took two steps toward the kitchen.

Sarah grabbed the back of Maddie's ridiculous sweater that showed Santa kneeling in front of a tree with a present, the jacket riding up to show his black thong. It wasn't an image I wanted to associate with anyone, especially Father Christmas.

"No, you don't." Sarah commanded. "I'm still hungover from yesterday's mulled wine, and if we start drinking now, we'll be passed out under the tree before the first guest arrives."

I nodded carefully, not wanting to rattle my wine-soaked brain too much. The extra sleep earlier had only alleviated some of the suffering. It'd been many months since I'd had such a wicked hangover.

"I'll go easy on the vodka." Maddie tried to wiggle free, but Sarah clamped on for dear life, causing Maddie to gurgle as if she were being strangled. Maybe she was. Sarah did hate when people deviated from her party battle plans. It was obnoxiously cute.

"I'm not buying that. Get to work." Mercifully, she let Maddie go before I had to contemplate whether or not to dial 911. I hadn't figured out whether I'd be requesting police for backup or an ambulance.

That was one Christmas memory I hoped to avoid.

Maddie, reaching for her neck, swiveled around to Sarah. "We're all hurting from yesterday. The best cure is the hair of the dog. Trust me." She tapped her fingers together in an evil sorceress way.

Sarah let out a bark of laughter. "I trusted you last night, and look how that turned out. I had to call Mom to come get the twins this morning because Lizzie and I couldn't function fully. I can't cancel Christmas because you don't know the proper vodka to tomato juice ratio. I'm not in my twenties anymore and am creeping scarily closer to forty every day."

Maddie waved a hand. "Nonsense. Rose loves swooping in to help you two out, and I'm sure the twinks are having a blast spending the day with their grandmother and Troy. He's probably on his thirtieth rendition of 'Twinkle, Twinkle Little Star.' The man loves that song." Maddie slanted her head. "Besides, I peeked at your plan. You'd already scheduled Rose to whisk the twins away to give us time to prep everything."

"Not before I got out of bed and that's not the point." Sarah massaged her forehead, clearly lacking her usual vigor when arguing.

"Let me put it this way; either you let me make some Bloody Marys, or I'm outta here. Or at least heading back to bed." Maddie charged into the kitchen before Sarah could strangle her for real.

Sarah locked her bloodshot eyes onto mine. "Don't encourage her."

I yawned and stretched my arms overhead. "I didn't say a thing."

"Exactly!" She stormed out of the family room.

I eyed the stack of boxes on the twins' art table. "How will I know who the recipient is?" As I was alone in the room, no answer was provided.

In the corner by the fireplace stood one of three full-sized Christmas trees in the house, this one overloaded with Disney ornaments since it was the tree the twins spent the most time by. The other two were in the living room and library.

I plugged in the bubble lights to gin up my festive spirit. Sitting at the table, with my knees jutting out since the chairs were toddler-sized, I selected the top box on the pile to my right. After careful examination, I spied Ollie's initials, ORP for Olivia Rose Petrie, in the upper righthand corner of the box. I grabbed one from my left and sure enough, it had FJP for Frederick James Petrie. Smaller piles in the middle had the names of other family and friends, as well as my name and Sarah's. I wasn't surprised to see my name on some of the boxes, since Sarah had been clear Maddie would be wrapping all of the gifts that didn't belong to the twins. And it wasn't the first time we'd done this. Sarah could be extremely practical that way.

But it was the first time she'd purchased her own gifts.

Maddie sashayed with extra pep, clinging to two glasses with celery stalks sticking out of the red liquid. "You haven't gotten very far."

"Sarah bought gifts for herself and wants us to wrap them." I accepted the glass but didn't take a sip.

"Okay." Maddie set hers on the table and scrunched down into a chair. "Let's get cracking." She took a hefty slug.

"You don't find it weird that Sarah got herself gifts?" I rattled one of the smaller, flatter boxes.

"Did you get her anything this year?" She crossed her arms over her chest in her typical accusatory way.

"Of course, I did." I tossed my hands up, annoyed she thought I'd forget to buy the mother of my children a Christmas gift.

Maddie crossed her arms. "What?"

"A necklace." I rattled the box again, but it didn't make much of a sound, giving me zero insight into the contents.

"Just a necklace?" Maddie took the box from me.

"Well, it goes around her neck so yes, I'd call it a necklace."

Maddie whacked my leg with the flat box. "Describe it."

"Oh." I palm-slapped my forehead. "It has a gold chain and an antique locket. That's why I asked for your help to select the perfect photo of the twins. It has a ruby and some other stuff. Um, it's elaborate." I tried miming the intricacies of the design but gave up. "I have no idea how to describe the scope or pattern. It's old."

Maddie appraised me with one eye closed. "That means it was expensive. When in doubt, you always go for flash, like when selecting wine in a fancy restaurant."

"You could say that. About the necklace, I mean." I remembered the money I'd forked over.

"How expensive?" She widened her eyes, waiting for me to fill in the blank.

"Let's put it this way. One of the twins may not be able to go to college." I laughed. "Totally kidding, but I think Sarah will love it." I rattled another box in Sarah's pile.

Maddie nodded appreciatively. "Did you happen to go shopping with Gabe? In the ring department? That might be a good sibling thing for you two to do."

"Why would I buy Gabe a ring?" I took the tiniest of sips of the Bloody Mary, hoping Maddie's *hair of the dog* theory was true. With Sarah's foul mood and Maddie's inquisition, this wasn't the time to have foggy-brain syndrome.

"Not buy *him* a ring. *Help* him buy a ring." She exaggerated the key words with her typical southern dramatic flair.

Catching on, I still couldn't help myself. "Is he wanting a ring?" I snapped my fingers. "Hey! Why don't you get him one? I'm sure the shops are still open. You might even be able to have something delivered. Money makes the world go 'round."

Maddie stared at me with her mouth slightly agape. "Are you fucking with me?"

Sarah dashed into the room on a mission. "I don't hear any wrapping. Less talk. More work." She pantomimed we should close our traps and then disappeared into the kitchen.

"I bet she's hitting the Bloody Mary." Maddie cupped her ear. "Yep." She looked way too pleased about her victory.

I grabbed one of Freddie's boxes. "You heard the boss. Get wrapping."

Maddie reached for one of Ollie's. "Maybe I *should* get Gabe a ring. Why do I have to wait for him to get his act together? As my grandfather used to say, *It's time to shit or get off the pot*."

I cut the wrapping paper, covered with penguins wearing scarves and Christmas hats. "What are you talking about?"

"Asking Gabe to marry me."

I held the scissors aloft, the sharp end pointing in her direction. "Really? I wasn't aware you wanted that with anyone. Not after ditching Peter at the altar."

"What does that have to do with this?"

I waggled the scissors before I realized I was shaking a sharp object at her. Setting them to the side, I asked, "Is this a trick question? Like some logic puzzle on the GREs."

"I don't see how ditching one man at the altar for cheating means I don't ever want to get married."

"And you want to now? To Gabe? After dating less than a year? I hadn't realized your relationship had progressed to… this. Isn't this something lesbians do?" I was babbling, which I did when unsure what to say. Maddie's decision had a whiff of desperation to it. Admittedly, I'd been told on numerous occasions that I wasn't the most romantic or observant of those around me.

"It feels right to me. I can't explain it." She leaned over the table and whispered, "Would it be weird for me to ask him?"

I placed a hand on my chest. "You're asking me? Do you not remember how I proposed to Sarah? It involved an insect bite, resulting with a ring being cut off of her swollen finger, and Sarah forcing me to buy her a diamond ring the next day all while on a weekend trip to New York City."

"I prefer hearing that story from Sarah. She makes it sound so much more romantic. Like her crying when the ER doctor told her he had to cut off the ring and you promised to buy her a new ring because she was so upset."

"You haven't wrapped one gift yet?" With five massive steps, Sarah loomed over us, her clipboard held in an intimidating head-bashing manner.

Not that I thought she'd whack me with it, but to be safe, I babbled, "Maddie's going to ask Gabe to marry her."

Maddie tossed a silver bow at me. Much more preferable than a clipboard. "Rat!"

"I wasn't supposed to tell Sarah? You tell her everything," I said, more baffled than if she demanded I tell her the square root of 1,974.

"Are you going to get on one knee? Should I add the proposal to the schedule? Before or after caroling? Or while caroling? It's supposed to snow tonight, so it'll be super romantic." Sarah clicked her pen, waiting for Maddie's input.

Maddie showed her palms, scooting back in her chair, nearly toppling over backward. "Hold on. I haven't decided if I'm going to or not. I was just spitballing."

"About getting married?" Sarah sat on the edge of the coffee table, still clutching her clipboard in a way that made me skittish. "Marriage isn't something to toss out willy-nilly. It's a commitment, twenty-four hours, seven days a week, every day for the rest of your life." A darkness clouded her eyes. "Do you *have* to get married?"

Maddie threw Sarah some serious shade. "Are you asking if I'm pregnant?"

I was having a hard time getting a read on the sudden hostility between the two. Maybe I should pour the rest of the booze down the kitchen sink. Right after I took a healthy slug. And another. I never drank on the holidays when I avoided family time. Liquor stores must make a killing this time of year.

Maddie slanted her head. "What's really going on with this?" She circled a finger in front of Sarah's face. "Why the bitchiness? And don't blame it on the hangover. You've been acting slightly off for the past few days, and I don't think it's just the holiday bash."

Now that Maddie mentioned it again, Sarah had been barking at Maddie more than me. And asking me to go to Hobby Lobby—that was just weird. Was that why she'd purchased herself Christmas gifts? Retail therapy? I had zero intention of posing these questions to Sarah, who looked as though she regretted not strangling Maddie earlier. Aside from the commitment, another aspect about marriage was knowing when not to confront an already irritated wife. Especially when said wife had a clipboard in her hands. Not to mention all our loved ones were expected in hours. This wasn't the hill to die on.

"Have not." Sarah swiped my drink and nearly finished half the glass in one gulp.

"Why don't I get another round?" I rose, retrieving both glasses.

On the kitchen island, a raw turkey sat in a pan, ready to go into the oven. "I'll trade places with you, buddy," I said to the bird.

"Who are you talking to?" Sarah placed the clipboard on the counter.

"What?" I turned around and offered a smile. "Oh, no one. When does the turkey need to go in?" It was best to keep her focused on the upcoming dinner, not on whatever was going on between her and Maddie.

She pulled her phone out of her pocket. "Four hours and forty-seven minutes."

I retrieved the pitcher from the fridge. "Would you like more?"

She started to say no but then nodded her assent, casually glancing over her shoulder to see if Maddie was near.

I filled her glass almost to the brim. "Are you okay?"

"We're two hours behind schedule." She hugged her chest.

It was difficult to determine if it was the party or something else, considering the party was for family and our closest friends who couldn't care less if everything went according to schedule. More than likely, they'd probably appreciate if the schedule was tossed out completely. At any rate, I didn't think it pertinent to bring this up.

"Okay." I set her drink on the countertop, yanked her arms apart, and held her in mine. "What can I do to kick things into a higher gear?" I released Sarah and swiped one palm along my other to give the impression of mock speed.

Sarah parked on one of the barstools. "Troy's going to pop the question."

I blinked.

Maddie entered the kitchen. "What's taking so long with the beverages?"

"Troy's going to pop the question," I said in a robotic voice.

Maddie pivoted to face Sarah. Shaking an accusatory finger, she started to speak with way too much joy in her tone and a slight hop. "That explains your weirdness!" Maddie claimed the barstool next to Sarah's. "What clues are there to make you think he's going to do that? Has he moved in officially?" Was she asking for herself? Wondering if she missed anything about Gabe?

Should I pull Gabe aside and fish? Prod? Warn?

"He asked for my permission," Sarah said. "They're talking about him moving in after the holidays. He thinks they should be engaged before the movers arrive. Ticktock."

How did I not know this? Sarah wasn't one to keep secrets. That had been my thing.

Buying her own gifts.

Not telling me this.

I didn't like any of it.

Or had I not been available with the end of the semester craziness? She always tried to shield me during my stressful times, given stress could cause a thyroid storm, which would threaten my remission from Graves' disease.

Again, I didn't like Sarah feeling like she had to shoulder this and the party all on her own. We were a team, dammit.

"And?" Maddie asked, appropriating one of the Bloody Marys on the counter.

Troy, many years Rose's junior, wanted to marry Sarah's mom, who had been single since Sarah was a toddler. And Sarah hadn't warmed up to them dating until very recently. It was one of the few times I'd witnessed Sarah acting like a Petrie: pigheaded and in the wrong. The mere idea sent my head spinning. Now he wanted to take the relationship to the next step when reaching the current step, dating, had sent Sarah into a tailspin. They'd only met this year. Granted, Rose wasn't getting any younger—*mental note, Lizzie. Don't say this aloud, especially to your mother-in-law, who recently warmed to you after you broke Sarah's heart in the past.*

"What?" Sarah either didn't hear the question or was stalling. My gut said it was the latter.

"Did you give it? Your permission?" Maddie pressed in a more supportive tone.

Sarah stared blank-faced.

Finally able to command my body some, I asked, "Did you?"

"I... I guess. I said he didn't need my permission. If he wanted to ask Mom, he should." Sarah spoke with zero emotion, a terrible sign on a day when there already had been the *sugar with her morning coffee* clue something was off. This did not bode well for the rest of the day.

"But, it does impact you and me, kinda," Maddie said.

I gave her a *what gives* look. Maddie was self-involved, but this was taking it to a new level. Was she worried it would upstage her proposal to Gabe if she opted to take that route?

Sarah nodded, much to my surprise. "Our writing project, yes, I thought of that. But, would it really change things? He's practically living with my mom, and soon, he'll officially move in. I'm getting used to that."

Drat! I'd completely forgotten about their children's book collaboration. I made another mental note to ask how it was coming along, but the timing stank at the moment.

"Let's go into the family room, wrap gifts, and discuss this new development." Maddie motioned for both of us to get moving.

CHAPTER SIX

Around two, Rose and Troy arrived with the twinks, who were both wearing reindeer outfits.

Sarah clapped her hands together. "Oh goodness, you two are adorable!"

Ollie's expression was dubious at best, but Freddie's eyes lit up with Sarah's praise and he tottered into her waiting arms. Ollie tugged on the front of her outfit, and I was willing to bet it would only last for five more minutes, tops.

"I couldn't help it when I saw them online," Rose said. "How are things going here?"

"Better. Thanks so much for rescuing the twins and me this morning." Sarah gave her mom a hug, which still caught me off guard sometimes. My mom hadn't been the hugging type. More the *stab you in the eye with a salad fork if you asked her to pass the butter* type.

"You sounded rough. Am I correct in assuming Maddie was the culprit?"

Sarah and I nodded.

Rose laughed. "There's always one friend like her in a group." She shrugged off her jacket. "What can I help with?"

I almost tossed my arms around her neck and blubbered, "Thank you."

"With dinner." Sarah motioned I was on twin patrol while she and her mom charged to their kitchen battle stations.

Troy followed them.

Olivia had managed to wiggle one arm out of her reindeer outfit, her free arm lodged under her chin and the other still in the appropriate sleeve. Her holler was truly impressive, and I didn't jump into action right away, shocked Sarah and I had created this creature.

My mom instinct kicked in. "Let me help, baby girl." I hunched down and wrestled the picky toddler free. "You shouldn't let Grandma torture you like this."

The redness in her face seeped quickly, another factor of her personality that staggered me.

The next to arrive early was Gabe, who appeared in the family room with a dozen red roses for Maddie, his face slightly gray. The aftereffects of Maddie's mulled wine, perhaps? Sign of the flu? If he was getting ill, I'd love for him to give me his germs. I could use a few days in bed.

Maddie joined us. "How was your day?" She stood on tippy-toe to give him a kiss on the lips.

"I fixed the toilet." He evacuated to the kitchen on some mission he hadn't explained after thrusting the flowers into her chest.

Maddie started to speak to his retreating back but shook it off.

"Would you like a vase? We have a ton now since Sarah put in a weekly flower order from Helen's." I motioned to the roses.

"I'll get one." She took a step away and then whirled around with a finger in the air. "You didn't say anything to Gabe, did you?"

"Wh-when?" I stuttered, taken aback by her ferocity.

"Today?" She shook the roses as if that explained everything.

"Besides hi, no." I stroked my chin. "Why?"

"That was weird, right? Who says 'I fixed the toilet' when asked how their day was?"

"Someone with a broken toilet, I guess." I shrugged, not fully understanding her concern. Christmastime made many rational people act a little nutty. Maddie was case in point at the moment.

"I didn't even know his toilet was broken. Does he mean in the shop? His apartment?" She sounded angrier by the second.

Gabe reentered the room.

Maddie called him over. "Hey, you okay?"

A smile stalled on his face, turning into more of a grimace, and he said, "Sarah needs me in the garage." He fled toward the living room, which was the longest possible route to the garage.

Maddie eyeballed me as if everything was my fault.

I cupped my ear. "I think I hear the door." I bolted on the pretext of carrying out my duty of official greeter, even though the party hadn't started, and I wouldn't mind if the skies opened up and dumped three feet of snow within the hour, cancelling Christmas.

Sarah was in the living room, with Ollie on her hip.

"There are my beautiful girls." I kissed Sarah's cheek and Ollie's head. Leaning in, I asked, "Did you need Gabe's help in the garage?"

"No." She quirked her head in her *I need more details* way.

"For now, if Maddie asks, can you say yes? Think of something convincing."

"What in the world would I ask Gabe to do in the garage?"

"Garage things." I tossed a useless hand in the air. "Oh, what toilet was broken?"

Sarah goggled at me. Placing the back of her hand on my

forehead, she asked, "Are you feeling okay? You tend to get sick at the end of every semester. Your body simply crashes."

"God, I'd kill for the flu right now. The type that knocks you flat on your back and you don't remember entire days. Sadly, I feel fine." I filled Sarah in on the Gabe and Maddie situation in short, hushed sentences.

Sarah nodded. "It's not just the Petries who are determined to ruin holidays."

I hefted a useless shoulder again. "I swear I'm not. I will do everything I can to ensure your holiday goes according to plan."

"*My* holiday?" Her voice crescendoed.

I waved that wasn't what I meant, but the damage had been done.

Her eyes dug into mine.

"Where's Freddie? I should check to see if he needs changing." I absconded to the kitchen.

Sarah shouted after me, "We'll pick this up later."

In the kitchen, Rose was snuggled against Troy.

Fuck, did he just pop the question?

I could kill him.

I had to shake my head hard to dislodge that terrible thought. Did I really just think about murdering Troy? For being in love? On Christmas Eve?

"Hey there. Have you seen Freddie?"

"Are you saying you don't know where your son is?" Rose's face was aglow.

"Not at the moment. No."

She smiled. "Last I saw him, he was with Maddie heading upstairs."

"Thanks!" I took the stairs two at a time.

Maddie had Fred on the changing table. "When you grow up, Freddie, don't be anything like your uncle Peter or uncle Gabe. In fact, don't be like a guy."

Freddie cooed.

"Yes." She tickled his belly. "Always stay sweet for Aunt Maddie."

"Can I help?" I sidled up next to her.

"I'm educating your son about how to be when he grows up."

"That's a lot of pressure given he's not even two." I took over cleaning Freddie's bottom. "Why do you think Gabe's acting odd?"

"Maybe he found out I wanted a ring or something." She nudged my shoulder with a finger. "Are you sure you didn't say anything? You aren't good at these types of things."

"I've been with you all day."

"You can be sneaky when need be. You *are* a Petrie."

"The innocent one, besides this one." I secured Freddie's clean diaper, snapping his reindeer pants back in place. "There you go, little man." I held him in my arms. "Such a handsome reindeer."

Maddie straightened his antlers. "Maybe I gave him all the wrong hints."

"I'm assuming you mean Gabe, not Freddie." I kissed Fred's cheek.

Maddie leaned against the wall, her arms crossed. "The other day, I may have joked it was time to shit or get off the pot."

I laughed. "And I thought my proposal was the world's worst in the romance department. Maybe getting advice from your grandfather isn't the best course when it comes to relationships."

Ignoring me, she said, "It's just I see you and Sarah every day with your children. And it's what I want. I want to settle down. And I think Gabe is the one for me."

There it was again. A sign of desperation. Had her biological clock started to tick? Did that really happen to women? "Think or know?" I asked.

Maddie looked up from her feet. "Know." She clutched her sweater over her heart and pinched her eyes shut. "Did I ruin it? God knows I'm not getting any younger."

Was that her reason for wanting to get married? Simply the age factor? Was it the time to dissect it, though? With Sarah's party about to start? I maneuvered over to her, shifting Fred to my other hip so I could wrap an arm around Maddie. "It's going to be okay. Gabe loves you. Any fool can see it."

"Guys are weird, though. They're even more obtuse than you."

"If that's true, you're royally screwed," I deadpanned. "Maybe you can fake an insect bite or something à la Sarah. You can be pretty conniving when you put your mind to it. Getting your finger to swell—that might be tricky. Oh, you don't have a ring. That was key to Sarah trading in her amethyst for a diamond."

She laughed, some snot bubbling out. "Sometimes I hate you."

"I have that effect on most chicks."

She rested her head against my shoulder. "Don't tell Sarah about this. Not tonight. She's worked so hard."

I laughed. "If you think I can keep this from her, you are giving me way too much credit. But, for the sake of our friendship, I'll do my best to avoid the mother of my children on Christmas Eve."

"That would be great," she said without a hint of humor.

I huffed, but she didn't seem to hear it, so did it really count? "You ready to come downstairs?"

She shook her head. "I need to repair the damage." She circled a finger, indicating her makeup.

"See ya on the flip side." I turned to go. "Hey, it will be okay. I'm making it my personal mission to make everyone's Christmas dreams come true. And my track record with relationship issues is stellar."

"You are such a dweeb."

"Are you calling me socially inept in front of my son?"

"Anyone who pulls the definition of dweeb out of their asshole is most definitely socially inept."

"Harsh, man. Harsh. Consider your Christmas dream cancelled." I made a slicing motion with my finger.

* * *

One foot landed at the bottom of the stairs, with my other still on the last step when Gabe tugged on my arm, jerking his head toward the library. "Let's go in there."

With Reindeer Freddie on my hip, I followed, curious why Gabe wanted to have a powwow in my office.

Did he want to apologize for last night?

Tell me he was leaving Maddie?

Or some other catastrophe I hadn't thought of but would have to manage?

With one hand on the knob and the other on the door, he carefully shut the door without making a sound aside from the click of the latch.

"What's up?" I whispered.

Gabe took a deep breath and ran his hands through his hair. "I…"

I waited a few moments to see if he'd continue on his own but gave up and prompted, "You what?"

He cradled the back of his neck with a hand. "I don't know if I can do it," he mumbled more to himself than me.

With each passing second, Freddie, the tinier twin, got heavier and heavier. I motioned for Gabe to take a seat on the couch while I settled on the opposite one, with a wiggling Freddie in my lap.

"Is everything okay?" I asked Gabe.

He nodded, staring at the table between the couches.

Maddie had artfully fanned out my *History Today* journals and *Economist* magazines, which she knew I hated, but she *claimed* it was impossible to curb the designer impulse.

"He did it. Six times." Gabe jabbed a finger at Henry VIII's image on the cover of one of the journals.

Freddie reached for the journal, but I handed him a picture book that was in the magazine rack on the side of the couch. "Here you go, little man. This one is all yours to do what you want." Which included pawing, drooling, and overall destruction. And he was the gentle twin. Ollie had special powers when it came to massive destruction.

Gabe smiled. "I'd like to have a son. Or daughter. A child. Healthy. That's all I care about. I'm ready to start a family."

"I'm jealous you won't have to have your eggs sucked out of you to create one." I smoothed the errant blond hairs on the top of Fred's head as he'd wiggled out of the hood of his outfit. "I'd do it a million times again to have another Fred. Or Olivia."

"The rate I'm going, it'll never happen." He slumped against the back of the couch.

Cold panic stabbed my gut. Had he decided to get off the pot? I forced out a laugh. "You kids today. In such a rush to settle down." I continued laughing, hoping I could soothe his nerves.

He lurched forward to the edge of the cushion. "I do want to. Settle down, that is."

"With?" I licked my lips, saying a silent prayer he wasn't about to say he was dumping Maddie for a woman who'd make a proper mom, not one who wore Santa porn to a family dinner.

"Maddie, of course. I"—he dug into his chinos pocket —"have a ring. I just don't know what to do with it. I mean, theoretically, I know but not the actual mechanics. Asking. I don't know how to ask. What to say."

Good God! Was everyone planning on popping the question at my house this Christmas? I, at least, had the decency to do it far away from home and not trouble everyone. Or Sarah did. On the Maddie front, this was great news. An unsettled Maddie was a dangerous Maddie. On the Troy front, it was a ticking A-bomb. Would he follow suit and ask Rose after Gabe got to a knee or whatever? Did men still do that?

Then there was the issue of Gabe and Maddie not dating all that long and the niggling feeling they were rushing. Each had mentioned wanting a family—a new development for both. Marriage, though, involved so much more than that. And, what would Helen think of her son marrying Maddie, who was a handful of years older than Gabe and who'd also left Peter at the altar? Helen was all for Rose's relationship with the much-younger Troy, but would it be different when it came to her firstborn?

Not noticing my internal turmoil, he asked, "How did you pop the question? Or did Sarah?"

"Neither of us did, really. It all just kind of happened." His face creased, so I rushed to explain. "You see, there was this spider and it bit Sarah's ring finger, which caused it to swell. They had to cut it off—the ring. Not her finger."

Gabe gaped at me as if I was a demented Mrs. Claus trying to kill all of Santa's elves.

"There you are." Sarah craned her head around the door, which she'd only opened partway.

I waved for her to come in and close the door, which she did.

Approaching us, she said, "What's wrong?"

Everything! I was in over my head. I waved my hand over my head to explain without words.

Gabe flourished the blue Tiffany box.

Sarah covered her mouth with both hands to muffle a happy squeal.

"He's asking for my help about how to pop the question." I yanked on the collar of my sweater. "Is it a hundred degrees in here?" I leaned forward to peer into my son's face. "Fred, are you hot?"

Sarah's smile revealed she knew me better than anyone else in the world. "Go. Leave us to chat." She put her arms out for Freddie, who was engrossed in the zoo board book. After handing him off to Gabe, Sarah walked me to the door. "Don't say a word about this to anyone. Especially Maddie."

"Avoid Maddie." I raised a finger. "Got it." I fled to the kitchen on the pretense that I needed to check the turkey. Had Sarah even put it in the oven? She'd mentioned it needed to go in at a certain point, but I'd lost track of time.

En route, the doorbell rang. "Got it!" I shouted to no one in particular, but it made me feel like a woman of action. Sarah wanted a perfect Christmas, and come hell or holy water, I'd make that happen.

I swung the door open.

"We're early," Ethan announced in a surly voice.

"Mom left us," Casey said.

"Uh... what?" This was the last thing I needed on top of Gabe's flip out and the Troy proposal bobbling on the surface of the Petrie shit wave. True, Ethan's marriage had been teetering on the edge of destruction, but leaving on Christmas Eve... Only a sociopath would do that. So far, my tally included two possible marriage proposals and one heading for divorce court. And the party hadn't officially started. Who knew what would happen when Peter and Tie arrived?

"Her mother is in the hospital," Ethan hurried to explain. "She's flying there now."

"And our house is boring," Casey added without much concern for her ailing grandmother.

My heart settled some, but one glance into Ethan's eyes behind his thick lenses made the uneasiness swirl again.

"Nothing but excitement here," I said in what I hoped was a confident and jolly voice.

"You have Netflix. That's all I need. We cancelled our account." Casey waved toodles on her way to the family room.

I gave my attention to Ethan. "Everything okay? With you and Lisa?"

"Is Maddie here? I need one of her eggnogs." He wringed his hands.

"Family room." It seemed best to let it go for now.

* * *

IN THE KITCHEN, I opened the oven door to check out the turkey, despite not knowing the positive or negative signs regarding cooking anything, especially a twenty-pound bird. As it turned out, the turkey wasn't in the oven yet, making my pretend task much easier.

"Are Ethan, Lisa, and Casey here? It's not even four." Sarah asked, checking her watch to ensure the party time hadn't actually arrived, or so I assumed. "I thought I heard their voices."

I shut the oven door. "Casey wanted to watch Netflix."

"And?" She tensed her shoulders as if knowing something was on the horizon. It seemed to be the theme of the day so far.

"And Lisa isn't here. She's flying home to see her mom, who may or may not be in the hospital. Not sure I'm buying the whole story."

"Oh, dear. This isn't good." Sarah hugged her chest.

"I know. I'll do my best to keep Ethan's drama from ruining your night."

"Lizzie!"

Fuck, I knew better from earlier. "What, sweetheart?" I replied in my cutest tone possible, which I hoped conveyed, *Please go easy on me; I'm doing the best I can.*

Sarah took in a sharp breath. "Ethan is our friend, and his

marriage is on the rocks. Do you really think I'd put my plans above that?"

I had, which clearly was the wrong answer given her flared nostrils. "Of course not. I was just... shit." I palm-slapped my forehead. "I need to help Gabe in the garage. I just remembered."

Sarah grabbed my arm as I tried to make my escape. Much to my surprise, she kissed me deeply.

"What was that for?" I asked.

"For being you."

"That's one of the nicest things you've said to me today."

"Because I've been too much of a taskmaster, you mean."

I simulated slamming my head into a wall.

She laughed. "Go before you dig a deeper hole."

"I adore you. You know that," I stated and planted a kiss on her cheek.

* * *

"LIZZIE, COME HERE!" Maddie shouted from the family room one hour after Ethan's arrival when I was starting to con myself into believing I could avoid all the guests for the remainder of the day if I pretended to dash about doing party things. Keep moving. Never talk.

My instructions from Sarah had been clear about not alerting Maddie to the impending proposal, but how could I not respond to Maddie without raising her suspicion?

Bullying my nerve to be cool, calm, and collected, I waltzed into the family room. "You bellowed, Maddie dear."

Maddie looked at me and then turned to Ethan. "She's hiding something."

"Am not!" I winced when my voice cracked.

Ethan, wearing a sweater depicting Santa on the toilet, grinned. "I think you may be right, *Maddie dear*," he mimicked.

Ah, my delivery blew my cover. *Stay calm, Lizzie.* They knew nothing.

Both of their faces were flushed. "Are you two drunk?" I got closer and took a whiff. "Yuck," I waved a hand in front of my face. "You smell like rum and stale cigarettes. Are you smoking again?" I asked Ethan.

He shook his head solemnly, making it loud and clear that was a resounding yes.

"Ethan! Lisa hates when you smoke."

"Lisa hates everything about me these days. Or haven't you noticed she's not here on Ch-Christmas Eve?" He wobbled on his tall legs.

Reining in the desire to shout "Timber!" I opted for, "Oh, Ethan. You two will work it out. Just give her time." I didn't believe a word I was saying, but how could I tell my stubborn, catty, and fluid-adverse best friend that he was impossible to live with and quite frankly I was surprised he'd stayed married for as long as he had? He should chalk it up as a win and focus on being the best father on the planet. Prioritize. Clear goals helped me survive day to day.

Ethan clamped his hand on Maddie's shoulder, all his fingernails perfectly trimmed and buffed. "Don't ever get married, Mads. It's not worth it. Marriage is the death knell for any relationship and crushes your soul." He touched his free hand to his chest with his dramatic flair, although his inebriated state made the action much clumsier than normal.

My mind boggled with the turn of events. First, Maddie pondering popping the question. Second, Gabe hiding in the library, or possibly the garage again, with an actual engagement ring. My car did need an oil change. Was he an oil change kind a guy? Maybe I should ask. It could give him a viable excuse to hide, and the more guests who didn't interact today the better.

Forcing my mind back on track, I listed the third event: Ethan advising Maddie not to get married because it'd ruin her.

Oh, wait, there was still the *Troy wanting to pop the question to Rose* issue that Sarah was struggling with. And the troublesome members of the Petrie family hadn't even arrived yet. What was it about the holidays that made everyone lose their frigging minds and then come over to my home and dump their relationship shit into my lap when all I wanted to do was make sure my wife's planning went off without a hitch?

My social skills were not equipped for this. Not at all. Yet, my friends and family were constantly straining my abilities. Why did they assume I had all the answers or the ability to help them navigate life's tricky waters? Sarah. The twins. We were an effective unit, and the glue was my darling wife.

There was a loud commotion in the living room, and part of me secretly hoped Hank had toppled the tree again, giving me an excuse to put all the ornaments back on and repair whatever damage had been done to the elaborate Dickens village, which spilled out several feet from the base of the tree, taking up a third of the living room. That type of diversion could take the rest of the evening. God knows it took me a full day to set up the tree and village according to Sarah's specifications. The village, which had some houses on books under the white sheet covered with fake snow, even included an ice pond that moved skaters around on magnets.

The doorbell rang.

"The doorbell! Someone's here. I should let them in. It's the doorbell," I blathered, dashing for safety.

I glanced over my shoulder to see if anyone in white coats was trailing me. Clearly, I was one step from insanity, never to return.

CHAPTER SEVEN

On the porch, Peter and Tie stood awkwardly with as much space between them as the small entryway allowed. My gut said they'd just finished another epic marital spat or had called an uneasy truce to whatever battle had brewed on their hour drive from Denver to Fort Collins.

Peter, red-faced and lips pursed, gripped Demi's car seat, his daughter fast asleep.

"Merry Christmas," I said with forced glee. "Don't you just love this time of year? The joy? Happiness? Family time?" With a wave of a hand, I said, "Come on in. Grab yourself some eggnog, and enjoy." *And if you could avoid screaming at each other, speaking to Maddie about the pitfalls of marriage, or anything else that could tip the already fraught evening into the deep end of batshit crazy, that would be much appreciated.*

I ushered them to the left so they'd be on the other side of the house, nowhere near Maddie or Ethan, and I was contemplating cordoning them off from each other in two of the rooms upstairs for the remainder of the evening.

The bell rang again.

Painting on my *everything's fine* expression, I opened the

door. "Dad! Helen! Allen! Come on in. Isn't this a magical evening?" Before shutting the door, I poked my head outside. "The snow has started, and it's really coming down. That'll be great for caroling, which is on the schedule for seven." I tapped my Timex.

Helen and Dad exchanged a quizzical look but didn't say anything.

"There's eggnog and hot cider in the kitchen. Snacks are in the dining room. Gabe's—" I stopped myself from saying either hiding in the library or the garage, trying to figure out how to pop the question. "In heaven. Not"—I pointed toward the ceiling with both hands. "I mean he's happy… that it's Christmas. Not for any other reason." I waved my hands frantically in the air. "No siree. Everyone is in a festive mood. Let's get this party started." I conjoined my hands, praying for this night to end without a major mishap.

Now Allen, who was usually as clueless as I was and missed most social clues, was staring at me like I was a frenzied Christmas elf.

Before he could say anything, Helen ushered the men away from me, maybe fearful my insanity was catchy.

I rested my forehead against the back of the door, enjoying the coldness against my flushed skin.

"That was terrible. Even for you." Sarah, with Ollie on her hip, smiled.

"I don't know what's wrong with me. For years, I was able to keep secrets. Now, with the knowledge Troy and Gabe are both planning to pop the question, the Maddie and Ethan situation developing in the family room, and Peter and Tie at each other's throats"—I scouted the entryway to see if any unwanted ears were near—"I'm losing my shit."

Sarah's eyes glimmered with happiness. "I can see that. Take Ollie. She needs to be changed. I'll see what I can do about the Maddie-Ethan thing."

"Thank God!" I got a whiff of Ollie's diaper during the transfer. "This will take a while!"

Sarah's eyes narrowed. "You seem way too chipper about a nasty diaper."

Maddie appeared like the Ghost of Christmas Past. "Have you seen Gabe?"

"Who?" I squeaked.

Sarah stepped in front of me, giving me cover to sprint upstairs to attend to Ollie under the guise of a catastrophic diaper situation.

I overheard Maddie say, "She's acting weirder than normal."

In the safety of the nursery, I whispered to Ollie, "Little girl, I may need your help tonight. Any time you need a change, just give me a shout." I placed her on the table, unsnapped the bottoms with dancing reindeers—the second outfit for the day after her earlier breakdown—and lifted her bum to attend to the disaster zone. "Now that's some serious poopage."

"Pooo…" Olivia giggled, reaching for her toes.

"Yes, poop. You did a poop." I yanked more wipes from the container. "Lots and lots of poop. You weren't dipping into Aunt Maddie's eggnog, were you?"

Ollie stopped giggling as if to ponder the question. Or to think of a lie.

"I'd never give a one-year-old eggnog. At least not with rum."

I closed my eyes and let loose a string of curse words in my head. "Who knows with you?" I glanced over my shoulder to see Maddie holding Demi. "Another situation?"

Maddie's pinched face was the only answer I needed.

"Here. Finish up with Ollie, and I'll take care of Demi."

Demi cooed.

I placed her on Fred's changing table. "Yes, my little Demi, let's get you cleaned." I tweaked her nose.

Maddie affixed Ollie's diaper and snapped her bottoms back

into place. Instead of taking her back downstairs, she sat in one of the rocking chairs, cradling Ollie close. "I don't think I can do it."

"What?" I got Demi's diaper off without gagging too much, something I didn't think I was capable of until I had twins.

"Ask Gabe to marry me."

You won't have to.

"Why's that?" I focused on the cleaning task at hand to avoid saying something I shouldn't.

"I'm not sure marriage is for me. Look at Ethan."

Since I had my back to her, I quietly released a cleansing breath and then ventured into the danger zone. "I'm not sure Ethan is the best to dispense marriage advice. He's a special case. You know this."

"He's married, though." Maddie said it as if Ethan was the only rational person she'd listen to about the subject.

"Yes. Lots of people in this world are married. Getting married doesn't automatically qualify you as an expert in relationships. Right, Demi?" I kissed the bottoms of her pink feet. "I'm going to eat your feet."

"Ffffftt." She giggled, releasing a spray of spit bubbles.

Ignoring Demi's cuteness, Maddie continued. "But Ethan's miserable. What if Gabe and I get married and I end up like that? And let's not forget, as you mentioned earlier, the last time I was engaged, I dumped the groom on our wedding day. I don't have the best track record when it comes to nuptials. And said humiliated groom is currently downstairs. The whole thing is messed up. What's wrong with me? Why did I think a relationship with Gabe could work out? Happiness isn't for me. Nor are relationships."

And why come to me about this?

Channel Sarah, Lizzie.

I snapped Demi's pants back in place, swept her into my

arms, and flipped around to see Maddie's red-rimmed eyes and Ollie's uncharacteristic worried expression.

Now what?

I took a seat in the rocking chair next to hers. "I'm not sure you should focus on your engagement with Peter, which had issues—"

"He was cheating on me. You can say it."

I turned my head to meet her combative eyes. "Do you think Gabe is cheating on you?"

"No." Her voice was meek, and her eyes zeroed in on the pattern of Ollie's blond hair that went every which way.

"Do you think he's the cheating type?"

"No, but what if down the road, he does? Or I do? There's no guarantee—"

"There isn't with anything in life. Not just marriage," I cut her off. "I can get creamed by a semi while riding my bike tomorrow."

"You aren't helping." She rested her head against the wooden chair.

"What do you want me to say? That no one in your marriage would cheat? I can't. That you'll always be happy. You won't. But I can tell you, you won't know if marriage is right for you until you try." She seemed unmoved, so I added, "Look at Sarah and me. We have a happy marriage, at least seventy percent of the time. Two beautiful kids. A house full of crazy family members and friends intent on destroying Christmas, but I wouldn't change it. This is life. This is family. You can take it or leave it. But ask yourself what you'll gain if you never step outside your comfort zone." I squeezed her thigh. "And, take it from someone who knows; staying a party of one out of fear is the loneliest feeling."

Maddie remained quiet.

Laughter and beginning chords of "Silent Night" from downstairs trickled into the nursery. I stood, placing Demi on my hip. "I should get back downstairs. You want to hang out here for a bit with Ollie? She's a great thinking buddy."

She shook her head, eliciting a smile from Ollie. "Do you want more eggnog, Ollie Dollie?"

"I knew it!" I feigned being outraged, placing my free hand on my empty hip, and gave Maddie my best hairy eyeball.

Maddie got to her feet, a little slower than usual. "You know, Lizzie, when I least expect it, you can offer semi-decent advice."

I placed Demi's hand over my mouth, speaking through the tiny splayed fingers. "Don't tell anyone. With the madhouse downstairs, I'd be huddling with different peeps all night dishing out Lizzie pearls of wisdom. Life is *so*"—I stressed this word, adding a gazillion Os—"much easier when everyone thinks you're a moron." I kissed Demi's fingertips, receiving the most wonderful laughter in return.

* * *

Downstairs, Helen pried Demi from my hip. "Ethan's looking for you." She jerked her head in the direction of the library.

"My work is never done," I whispered to myself as I stomped off to the kitchen to fix a cup of eggnog, knowing deep in my bones I'd need liquid courage.

Ethan paced from one bookshelf on the south side of the room to the other. "She's not answering my calls or texts."

"Who?" I asked in slim hopes he'd fall for it, and part of me prayed he'd say Mrs. Claus.

He growled at me, pivoting like a soldier on the parade ground, and headed off in the opposite direction, but only a few feet before he reached the furthest point.

My go-to of playing dumb obviously wasn't going to cut it.

"How's Casey taking it? Being away from her mom on Christmas Eve?" While her dad fumed in my library?

"She's Casey. Too wise for the rest of us." He waved a limp hand in the air.

I perched on the arm of the couch nearest to the exit. "I'm sure it's still hard for her. Being intelligent doesn't shield you from this." I waved to his approaching form, slightly intimidated by his grimace and sheer height.

"What do you want me to do?" he said through gritted teeth. "My marriage is falling apart. It's not like women are lining up to be with me. Lisa," his voice cracked. "She's the only one who ever understood me. Accepted my quirks."

I nodded, knowing he was speaking the truth.

"But, I can't just give in to Lisa all the time to keep her in my life." His expression morphed into steely resolve, which looked like it took great effort to accomplish. "We're barely surviving financially with just one child. I wake up in the middle of the night in a panic, wondering if the electricity or gas is still on. Or if we'll be able to afford groceries on Saturday. Every time my debit card is swiped, I hold my breath, waiting for it to go through. Student loans, mortgage, insurance." He stopped mid-step and turned to me. "What if one of us gets sick? Really sick and our health insurance won't cover the treatments? Then what?" He placed both hands on top of his head, straining to breathe, and the color drained from his face.

Was he in the midst of a panic attack?

I set my eggnog on the coffee table and hopped to my feet, ushering him to a seat. He reached for my drink, but I preempted him by asking, "Do you need some water?"

He nodded.

I retreated to the bar and grabbed a bottled water from the mini-fridge. "Here." I squatted, placing a hand on his thigh.

Ethan twisted the cap off the Evian bottle and gulped the

cold water. Wiping his mouth with the back of his hand, he said, "I don't know what to do. Tell me what to do."

"Have you talked to Lisa about all this?"

He raised his left shoulder. "Some of it."

"I think it's time you two had a full-on reckoning. Lay out all of your worries. She can do the same. But, Ethan, you shouldn't be the only one shouldering all the financial worry. You and Lisa are a team. Both of you work. Both of you should go over the finances together. Let her in to shoulder some of this."

He balked. "Why should she be as stressed as I am all the time?"

I peered through his coke-bottle glasses. "That's life and marriage."

"She doesn't handle money matters well." He clung onto the water bottle like he was afraid some force would strip him of it.

I bobbed my head. "Well, she's not handling you cutting her out, either. Is her mom really in the hospital?"

"Yeah, I think so. We couldn't afford the airfare for all of us to go."

Lisa's mom had been diagnosed with emphysema right after Thanksgiving, another reason why Lisa would be furious with Ethan for smoking.

"I get that. Does she know that's why you're here with Casey instead of with her during this trying time?"

"Casey wanted to be here. She refused to go before I even said we couldn't afford it. Lisa's parents are… protective, and with everything that's going on…" He left the rest unsaid.

I hadn't met them, but if they suspected Ethan and Lisa were on the rocks, I imagined they'd make things even more difficult, either by trying to interfere or taking Lisa's side, putting Casey in the middle of the feud.

Not wanting to get into that topic, I said, "We love having

Casey, but shouldn't Lisa know the truth? Do you really want her to think Casey prefers being here? And what about you? What excuse did you give her for you staying behind, knowing Sarah and I would have welcomed Casey with open arms? Lisa has to be wondering why you aren't there."

"Someone has to look after our daughter." His voice was brusque.

I groaned. "Please tell me you didn't put it that way."

"W-well, it's true," he stuttered.

"Partly true." My knees were killing me from squatting, so I sat on the couch next to him. "You of all people know how dangerous it is to keep things from your spouse. How many times have you counseled me on this very topic?" I nudged his leg with mine. "Ethan, you have to talk to her."

He reached into his jeans pocket to retrieve his phone. "How, when she won't answer my calls?"

"Do you really think this is the conversation to have over the phone? When she gets home and recovers from dealing with her mom's illness, sit her down and show her the numbers. Tell her how scared you are about financial ruin and the things you haven't told anyone else, including me. And"—I squeezed his thigh—"this will be the hard part since you always think you're right, listen to what she has to say. Maybe things aren't as bad as you're making them out to be."

"Says the woman who has more money than God." He took a tug of water, slopping some onto his sweater.

"Uh, that brings me to a touchier subject. You know, if you ever need any—"

He held up a hand. "I'm not taking any of your money."

We locked eyes. "Fine. I'll give it to Casey. She'd probably invest it in the next rage and rake in millions."

"If only I'd invested in Bitcoin."

"One of my greatest regrets as well," I mocked.

"Do you even know what it is? Just a few years ago, you

were listening to audiobooks on cassette until Sarah purchased an iPod and uploaded your books and her music for you." He jabbed his elbow into my side.

"Now I have a Kindle and have mastered one-click purchasing." I demonstrated with my finger.

"La-di-da!"

"Welcome back. Now let's go out there and spread some fucking Christmas joy!"

CHAPTER EIGHT

Peter and Tie, along with Rose and Troy, stood near the Christmas tree in the living room. The fire behind the glass doors roared, and the orange and red flames reflected in Tie's eyes, reminding me of a devil flick Maddie and Sarah had watched recently. Was that a sign for how the holiday would go? Or was I imagining things knowing Tie's propensity for stirring shit as much as humanely possible?

Rose asked, "Do you two have any travel plans coming up for the New Year? I'm trying to convince Troy to fly to Italy over his spring holiday." She threaded her arm through Troy's.

This was news to me.

Was Italy the honeymoon destination? And, from what I remembered, Troy wasn't the best traveler. Motion sickness or maybe it was something else.

"Oh, Peter *works* way too hard." Tie stressed *works* and then turned to Rose. "You're so lucky you're only connected to the Petries via Sarah's marriage." Tie leaned in close with the pretense of whispering in Rose's ear but said loud enough for all to hear, "As you know, the Petries have issues with fidelity." She jerked her head toward my father and Helen, who were speaking with Allen and Gabe across the room. "Lizzie seems to be the only good egg in the family. Sarah is truly lucky."

My heart plummeted to the pit of my stomach, and both Rose and I avoided looking at the other. For years, Rose had loved to make engine revving sounds as a way to remind me if I hurt her daughter again she'd mow me down with her car.

Had Rose forgiven me completely now that I'd helped smooth the waters with Sarah after she started dating Troy? Or would Rose mention that before Sarah and I married I hadn't been as well-behaved as Tie implied?

Or did Tie know more than I thought? Was she about to plunge into my past to cause even more issues for the night, Tie-phoon style?

Peter bristled.

Troy said, "Uh, I do think I can make Italy work if we wait until summer. My therapist—"

"There you are. How is everyone?" Sarah looped her arm through mine.

There was dead silence.

I said, "We're talking about summer vacation plans. I think it's the snow making everyone dream of warm days in beautiful places."

"Oh, Lizzie. You crack me up. Always trying to smooth over everything that goes on in this family. Don't you get tired of lying and covering for everyone?" Tie forced her arm through Peter's. Was she mimicking Sarah? Rose? Or ruffling Peter's feathers with physical contact?

Sarah's eyes glanced over me and then pounced on Tie. "You know what, Tie, I could use your opinion about the turkey. Lizzie is useless in the kitchen, and I'm not used to cooking such a large bird."

Peter's laughter cut through the air. "Tiffany can't even heat up a can of beans. Good luck." He never referred to her as Tie, like the rest of us. Truth be told, he rarely called me Lizzie, my preferred method of being addressed.

Sarah was usually better at diversionary tactics, and I worried about the rest of the night.

Tie patted her husband on the cheek. "I'm not the one with a bun in the oven." She flipped around to Sarah. "I'd love to talk turkey with you."

The two of them left.

Peter swallowed, ran his hand through his hair, and then departed without another word.

I mulled over her reference to having a bun in the oven, but forced it from my mind, not having the mental bandwidth for yet another obstacle to the perfect Christmas. Could a Tie-phoon strike if no one paid her any attention? And would Peter be so stupid to get another woman pregnant? My eyes landed on my father and his second wife, who had been his mistress for nearly two decades. Oh God... Neither of us had great role models. That didn't excuse all, but it did have an impact on us, the unloved children.

Troy released a low whistle. "Is she always like that?"

"Yes. I should go help Sarah, but I don't know... about large birds." I stayed rooted in place as if physically unable to move.

"Trust me, Lizzie, my daughter will put her in her place. It's best to stay here. And..." She left the rest unsaid.

I didn't say anything either. Surely Rose caught the *bun in the oven* reference. Perhaps she was of the same mind—don't acknowledge. Not on Christmas Eve. Thinking that made me slightly queasy, but honestly, I didn't trust Tie. Or Peter. Why was this my problem?

Troy, probably sensing there was more to the conversation than he realized, started discussing the snow outside the glass veranda door. "It's really starting to come down. Do you think we'll still be able to go caroling? I'm really looking forward to it."

I wasn't.

I was tempted to create a fake emergency of some sort and kick everyone out. What would qualify? Some type of health quarantine, but it wasn't like I could conjure up Typhoid Mary to scare the bejesus out of everyone.

I wished I could just stand on a chair, whistle, and say, "All of you are being terrible. Leave."

Knowing my luck, the storm would force everyone to stay the night, and that was the very definition of Hell.

As an atheist, I didn't believe in Hell.

If there was one, though, it would be filled with Petries.

Maybe it would be best if we didn't have any more children.

But if we did, no way in hell would I let any of them marry or even associate with a woman like Tie. What in the world had Peter seen in her in the first place? They'd started off as an affair, while Peter was engaged to Maddie. Rule number one: never marry the mistress. They knew all the dirt and held resentments right from the start. But Dad and Helen seemed happy. Or had the excitement started to wear off now that they'd married? My brain was spinning like tires on ice, unable to grip anything solid.

Sarah returned minus Tie, and she jerked her head, indicating she wanted a word in private.

Rose placed a hand on my shoulder. "Families, Lizzie, can be so very hard."

Tell me about it.

I approached Sarah, brushing my lips against her cheek. "There's my lovely wife. How'd it go?"

"We need to keep a close eye on that one. She's up to something. I can't quite put my finger on it, but I have a feeling it's going to be epic."

"Do you want me to keep her by my side?"

Sarah gave me her *you are so adorable* smile. "Thanks but

maybe Ethan would be a good candidate. He has experience with angry women."

I laughed. "And you don't think I do?"

Sarah ignored my comment. "And Maddie. That's complicated..." She tapped a fingernail against her front teeth. "The Peter connection, obviously." Sarah wheeled about and left me in the dust. "Ethan, my dear, can you help me flip the bird?" Sarah added, "The turkey, I mean."

Sarah needed a new excuse to pull guests to the side for her little confabs. Even I was catching on to the turkey gambit, and I wasn't the type to catch on to things very easily. At least that was what everyone always said about me.

Tie sidled up to me all on her lonesome. "The house looks amazing. And all your trees, how much time did it take to decorate? Or did you hire someone like Maddie? That's what Peter does. And your father. They say the apple doesn't fall too far from the tree."

Another veiled reference to my past mistake?

I gulped, not willing to share the actual amount of time we'd spent getting the house ready. Sharing details with a she-devil was on my *never do* list. "Oh, Sarah is quite the organizer, and her battle plans make everything as easy as pie." I snapped my fingers for emphasis.

This was only a little white lie.

"I'm sure. The only thing your brother can plan—"

The doorbell cut her off.

"Oh, that's my cue. I'm the official greeter." I tapped my chest as if I wore a yellow vest with a name badge, like Wal-Mart greeters, saying, "My name is Lizzie. How can I help you?"

I swung the door open. "George. Gandhi. Welcome and merry Christmas." George, with his shiny dome, looked somewhat dapper in a wrinkled suit and polka dot red bow tie. Gandhi, his Yorkie, sported a bow tie with green polka dots.

George held Gandhi in his arms, and I patted the dog's head. "Don't you two look handsome?" I waved them in with a flourish of my arm.

After setting the dog down, George slipped out of his wool jacket, getting snow all over the oriental rug. Given the increasing amount pouring from the clouds, there wasn't much that could be done about that. "Thank you so much for inviting us over. Now that Gladys is with the Lord, these days are…" He left the rest unsaid, his dull blue eyes drifting to the family room. "You know Gladys would have loved having daughters like you two. Children were never in God's plan for us."

Considering I had two children who I'd lay my life down for, I didn't know how to respond.

George rolled on. "Have either of you considered getting married? I was quite the catch in my day. Had a good job. A full head of hair." He leaned in. "Ya know, people love to gossip on Whipple Street. Two young ladies living alone—you get what I'm saying."

I did, and I didn't.

Was George proposing marriage in some roundabout way?

I didn't think it was much of a secret on our street that Sarah and I were the token lesbian married couple with children. And George knew we were raising the twins together. He'd attended their one-year birthday bash last summer. I didn't remember explicitly informing him that Sarah and I were legally married, but did I really have to considering we had children together? Perhaps his memory or grip on reality was slipping, which made his addition to tonight's holiday bash precarious.

Honestly, what was it about Christmas that made everyone lose their goddamn mind?

George had recently become one of Sarah's projects, and from what I gathered, everyone on the street was content to let her take on the elderly widower, who on his best days seemed like the eccentric, forgetful, and batshit crazy uncle most people skirted at family dinners. Sarah, though, had a heart of gold. And the mere thought of the old man rattling around alone in his big house—was just too much for her to bear. For as long as I'd known Sarah, she and her mom adopted a family who was struggling financially and provided all the gifts and food for Christmas dinner. George, really, was an extension of this.

"Can I get you something to drink?" I asked in hopes of ditching the *you should marry me so the neighbors won't talk* conversation thread. Was it possible he was joking? Maddie loved to point out I was a tad socially inept. Maybe this was case in point.

"Got any whiskey? It's a bit nipple-ly outside."

I silently sucked in a deep breath. Would it be wrong to give George an extreme amount of whiskey on the off chance it'd make him sleepy? Maybe a large tumbler in front of the roaring fire with a cozy flannel blanket to help him drift off?

"You got it. Most everyone is in the living room." I pointed the way, despite the fact it wasn't the first time he'd been in our home for a celebration.

George undid Gandhi's leash, and the dog immediately took off like a shot, more than likely hunting for Hank, our cat. I understood Sarah's need to invite George. Mostly. What I didn't understand was why the invitation extended to his dog, who enjoyed tormenting my loveable feline.

I tried to send a psychic message to our furball to be on the lookout for a demented Yorkie.

George toddled off into the din of Christmas celebrations, and from what I could hear, Tie hadn't launched World War III quite yet. Regardless, I noticed Sarah had kicked up the music a notch or two. I bobbed my head along to "I Saw Mommy Kissing Santa Claus." If only I could arrange that, since it seemed like the least disturbing event that could happen over the next twenty-four hours.

In the quiet of the library, the only light emanated from Maddie's so-called Christmas tree that consisted of books stacked onto each other in the shape of the tree, with large white bulbs. I had to admit, even the Scrooge inside me appreciated the effort, and this was by far my favorite decoration in the house.

Standing at the bar, with George's drink, I was tempted to take a shot of grappa—a drink I'd never tried until my first date with Sarah.

Come now, Lizzie.

Getting blitzed wouldn't accomplish much.

My fingers traced the elongated neck of the bottle, which looked a lot like a beaker found in a science lab.

Again, my mind wandered back. On the date, we'd started at a coffee shop and then ended up having dinner in a quaint Italian bistro. That day had ushered in all of this. Her moving in. Buying this house. Having the twins. Had the grappa gotten the ball rolling on everything?

Sarah slipped into the room. "Are you hiding?"

"Maybe a little."

Her eyes lingered on my hand still resting on the bottle.

"I was just thinking of our first date," I confessed.

"When I got you drunk." Her eyes twinkled.

"Very drunk. And I had to teach the next day."

Sarah pressed against my side. "I don't regret that at all."

"I don't want you to. What do you say? Shall we have a teeny-tiny nip for old time's sake?" I tapped the top of the bottle.

Sarah grinned. "It may be the only way we survive the night."

I uncorked the bottle and poured two shots into the vintage glasses Sarah had recently purchased.

We clinked glasses but didn't take a sip right away. Our eyes locked on each other.

"Would it be wrong to take you here, right now?" I asked.

Sarah's giggle wasn't entirely innocent. "If we could and not risk getting caught by the likes of Tie, I'd bend you over your desk." She shot her drink, and I followed suit.

"Ya know, maybe next Christmas, if we don't have a little one yet or if you aren't *beached whale* status," I paused for the shoulder whacking I rightfully deserved, "I can take us on a holiday trip. Someplace relaxing."

"Like Jamaica?"

"Sure." I had been thinking of Breckenridge or Vail, but what the hell? If whisking the family away on a beach holiday saved us from Tie, Peter, and all the other bullshit swirling around, I'd launch us to Mars if I thought it possible to find a viable beach instead of instant incineration. "Maybe we can invite your mom to come along."

"To babysit one or two of the evenings?" She pressed her forehead to mine, staring into my eyes.

"Exactly." I sighed, remembering my purpose for being in the library. "I better get George his drink. He's a strange man, and I'm about eighty-seven percent certain he proposed marriage to one of us."

Sarah, pulling her head away, laughed. "Probably both. He seems like the type who'd be up for that. A harem of lesbians, although, two doesn't really equate to that, but in his mind…" She let her voice drift off for effect.

I pinched my eyes shut. "Oh please. There's already so much I wish I hadn't seen or heard today. Don't add that image to my already fragile mind."

"Years ago, Lizzie, I truly believed you were absolutely clueless. Not so much anymore." Sarah strutted out of the library with that extra twist of her hips that got my heart beating, making me regret not attempting to have my way with her moments ago.

In the living room, George was chatting with Maddie and

Ethan. A quick survey of the room confirmed Tie was nowhere in sight. Had Sarah decided not to put someone else on Tie-phoon watch? Afraid that would only rile Tie more?

"Here you go, George." I handed off the tumbler.

He took a swig. "Thanks, my dear. The hair of the dog is the best way to start the day."

Maddie cooed, wrapping her arm around his. "A man after my own heart. I said the same thing earlier today."

It had been a crazy day and I'd lost count of the hours, but I was certain it wasn't morning anymore, considering how tired I was and the simple fact the guests had arrived. Casually, though, my eyes found the clock on the mantle to confirm it was indeed evening.

George practically glowed, clearly enjoying Maddie's touch.

"Late night?" Maddie nudged George's shoulder in a conspiratorial way.

"Always. This old dog still has plenty of life." He stepped closer to Maddie. "You know what you need?"

"What's that George?" Maddie took a sip of her special eggnog concoction that had enough rum to strip paint off furniture.

"What Lizzie has with Sarah?"

"Marriage?" Maddie's voice hardened, and her shoulders stiffened.

So, he did know we were married.

"Exactly! Back in my day, a woman like you would be banging down my door. And some still want to hop into my bed. For you, I'd offer the whole tamale, but don't waste time. If you skip now, forever keep your trap shut."

Funny. Ten minutes earlier he had been propositioning me as if I needed a man to offer me protection from the gossiping Whipple Street Club. Had he forgotten that? Or did sweet George use his elderly status to say and do whatever the fuck he wanted and I was only just noticing this habit of his? This freewheeling didn't bode well for the rest of the evening, and he was the last guest we needed to add to our usual family gatherings from now on. My nerves couldn't handle the likes of George, clueless or not.

Ethan, his eyes glazed and distorted behind his thick glasses, asked, "How long were you married, George?"

George scratched his unshaved chin. "Oh, a month shy of fifty years."

Ethan whistled. "What was your secret for staying married so long?"

"Blackmail."

Ethan and Maddie gawked at the man, but I wasn't buying anything he said. Taking into account what I had learned about his ability to fabricate any scenario that suited his purposes, perhaps he wasn't fibbing and wholeheartedly believed the words coming out of his mouth. Did that make him more dangerous? Humorous? Just another nut in the adopted Petrie family?

"Who blackmailed whom?" Maddie asked, much more interested in the old codger now.

George aped he was keeping his lips locked. "But to answer your question, my dear boy, the key is not to marry a bitch. My brother—God, his wife was horrible. Always nitpicking. Jealous as a hellcat. You can't control a bitch."

Maddie choked on her eggnog and nearly dropped her moose mug with delicate antlers that already made it difficult to drink from. Only Sarah would buy something so useless, and I never had the heart to ask how much she'd paid for them.

Maddie said, "You're a naughty man, George."

Some life replaced the dullness in the edges of his eyes. "We can go across the street for me to show you just how naughty."

Ethan met my eyes as if inquiring if I'd heard that. Maybe he was wondering if he was hallucinating.

Unfortunately, I had absorbed every word, and I was certain

I could have lived a long and fruitful life without witnessing an old man attempting to seduce one of my best friends.

"I'll keep that in mind. It may be my best offer for the night."

I swiveled my head to Maddie, wondering if she'd consumed an entire bottle of rum without the eggnog.

She hitched a shoulder.

"Are you the jealous type?" George asked.

Maddie cocked her head. "Uh, I guess it depends on the situation."

I prayed she wasn't going to bring up that Peter had cheated on her and then married one of the women who'd wrecked Maddie's relationship. That woman stalked this party like a shark waiting for the first hint of blood.

"Because sometimes I love dick," George said without much emotion in his tone or body language.

The three of us remained speechless as if wondering whether what we heard was what he had said. Or at least that was what I was trying to figure out.

No wonder the other neighbors who had known George longer never invited him over.

"What about you, my boy?" George swirled his drink in Ethan's direction. "Do you know what I mean? We could make it a threesome."

I blinked.

Maddie chewed her bottom lip.

Ethan paled.

In grad school, he'd had a difficult time, and one of the main reasons was many thinking he was gay. Not that he was homophobic, but it seemed to needle him more than he cared to let on to me for the obvious reason.

Tie flitted over and joined the fray, and it may have been the first time since meeting her that I appreciated her intrusive presence.

"Tie, do you remember our neighbor George?" I said.

Tie bared the most beguiling smile. "I do. You were at the twins' birthday party."

Odd.

Tie usually pretended not to remember anything.

"What about you, darling? Do you like dick?" George asked.

I genuinely had no idea how to handle this situation.

Given Maddie and Ethan's horrified faces, neither did they.

Tie, though, grinned. "Oh my, finally some color to one of the Petrie parties." She hooked her arm through George's. "It looks like you need a refill, and I happen to know where Lizzie keeps the best whiskey."

She led him into the library.

My library.

My sanctuary.

"Uh, is Tie going to fuck George in my library?" I asked.

Maddie bobbed her head side to side. "There's a good chance she may."

"I may never be able to go in there again, and it used to be my favorite place in the house."

"I love you and Sarah, but these gatherings are getting weirder and weirder." Ethan downed his eggnog. "I need more. Anyone?"

Maddie handed off her moose mug.

I shook my head.

"I should go check on… I don't know. Something." I fled the room for a brief respite. Where, though? Many of the guests had congregated in the kitchen, while Sarah and Rose prepped more of the meal. Casey and Allen were in the family room working on a puzzle and watching *It's a Very Merry Muppet Christmas Movie* with the kiddos.

Where was Peter?

Maybe he'd requested a helicopter to save him from another night with Tie. Was every day of his life like this? Of course,

Peter had sown his own misery. I still didn't have the brain power to contemplate whether or not he had another child on the way with someone other than his wife. Conversely, I remembered Courtney warning me that Tie was planning something big to bring Peter down. Was Tie telling the truth? I hadn't been Peter's biggest fan the majority of my life, but if Tie was setting him up, I truly felt sorry for my older brother. If she wasn't fibbing, how would I take to the news, given the situation with my father?

Dad and Helen came downstairs, and my mind briefly flitted to figuring out why they had been upstairs. *Nope, not going there.*

I hummed along to *"Feliz Navidad"* as I opened the front door and stood outside for a breath of fresh air. The wind kicked up snow around me, and I wrapped my cardigan tighter around my chest. "What a fucking weird family."

A massive snowflake landed on my nose.

I looked up into the whiteness, trying to figure out if that was a sign or not.

A crunching sound caught my attention. I craned my head around and spied a man, without a jacket, pacing the snow-packed drive.

"Peter?" I called out as a burst of wind struck my face.

The person didn't turn.

I groaned. A minute or two out in the elements was what I wanted. Longer than that and I feared the elements. How, though, did I just go back inside and not check on who I was certain was my brother? He hadn't been the best sibling. Verifiably shitty. But he still was my brother and clearly not doing well. For the majority of his life, he'd had the Scotch-lady's protection. Now that she was dead and with the introduction of Dad's other family, including another son, Peter had been drifting further and further into the deep-end of shit he may not come back from. I went back and forth on whether or not I should be there for him. Deep down, I felt a connection to him.

We'd both been used by our mother in her quest to torture her husband.

Fuck it.

I approached. "Peter?"

He turned on his heel, the snow making a bone-crunching sound. A cigarette dangled on his bottom lip. "Oh, hey."

"What are you doing out in this without a coat?"

He smiled, kinda. "You really are becoming more and more mom-like each time I see you."

I laughed self-consciously. "Hopefully nothing like ours," I said, forgetting Peter had actually gotten along with her.

To my surprise, he nodded.

"So, what are you doing out here?"

"Thinking." He took a drag.

"About anything in particular?" I held my chest tighter, doing my damnedest to retain all my body heat.

He shrugged. "I'm not sure it matters anymore."

That was an odd answer and probably the least assuring. "Come on back inside. We can talk in the li—I mean by the fire in the living room. That'll help warm you up. Your lips are turning blue."

"I'm okay out here."

I shook my head. "No, you aren't, and I'm not taking no for an answer."

He sucked in a deep breath and narrowed his eyes. Taking one last drag, he flicked the lit cigarette off the side, the snow extinguishing the red tip on impact. "I need bourbon anyway."

Inside, Peter started to make way for the library, but I put my hand on his. "Let me get the bourbon. Go stand in front of the fire. No getting pneumonia on my watch."

Not putting up an argument, he showed me his backside on his way in the opposite direction of Tie and George.

With my hand on the library door, I wondered if I should knock before entering. What would be best, barging in and catching them in a compromising position or giving them advance warning and entering while they were hastily pulling on their garments? Did we have a spare bourbon bottle in the kitchen for cooking? Sarah and Maddie had made a banana cake or pie that called for it. But they used cheap bourbon. Peter would know if I didn't serve him Blanton's Original Single Barrel.

I opted to enter. It was my library after all, and as soon as I had it fumigated, I intended to block it off if we ever had the family over again. That was a huge fucking *if* at the moment.

I was done with the Petries, aside from my offspring and wife. And, I was in the mind frame of changing our last name.

All Sarah wanted was to have a nice family meal. All her hard work. Dedication. Even our neighbor George could torpedo everything with another "I like dick" comment.

I audibly groaned as I swung the library door open.

To my sweet surprise, the room was empty. Nonetheless, I purposefully didn't seek out any hidden spots.

And if she'd truly left the room, that meant Tie was on the loose again.

I fixed Peter's bourbon and contemplated another shot of grappa.

Skipping the grappa, I repaired back to the living room.

Most of the family members were sitting or standing in small groups in the warm room with the Echo Dot now playing "Silent Night," and it couldn't have been more ironic. I had to force down an insane bout of giggling or I feared being committed before night's end. Would that be so bad, though?

Sarah, with Ollie on her hip, beckoned with an almost imperceptible jerk of the head. Maddie cuddled Freddie in her arms.

I dropped off Peter's bourbon, leaving Dad and Helen to deal with him for the moment.

"Well, isn't this a sight?" I tweaked Ollie's nose and enjoyed the giggling sounds she made.

Freddie stared wide-eyed.

"Anything to report?" Sarah asked.

Where should I start? Tie and George possibly canoodling in my office, aka the library? Peter? Maddie and Gabe? Ethan and Lisa? "Uh, not a thing. How goes the battle plan for the rest of the evening?" I took Ollie from Sarah's arms. "Ollie, give Mommy a hug."

Ollie was kind enough to wrap her chubby arms around my neck.

"You give the best hugs." I snuggled her closer. "And you, little man, come here." I swiveled Ollie to one hip, and Maddie shifted Fred onto my free one. One sniff alerted me to the never-ending parenting duty of toddlers. "Let me take you two upstairs."

Sarah kissed my cheek. "Thanks, sweetheart. I was just about to do that."

"I'll go with you," Ethan said.

I nearly rolled my eyes, knowing Ethan wouldn't help at all with changing a diaper.

"Would you grab Demi?" I might as well put him to some use. I only had two arms.

Upstairs in the nursery, I placed Freddie in his crib, knowing he wouldn't squawk about the confinement like Ollie would. Fred enjoyed time to himself. Ethan cuddled Demi.

While changing Ollie, I asked, "What was that with Tie and George?"

"Who knows? And what was with George talking about liking dick? Did he have a stroke or something? I don't remember him being this odd the last time I spoke to him."

"Would a stroke do that?"

"It's been known to rewire the brain, making the person

you'd once known unrecognizable. How well do you know George?"

"I've had a few conversations with him about the weather and stuff. You know. The conversations you have when you bump into a neighbor but don't want to take the time to really try."

Ethan's observation alarmed me, and I had to admit, not for the right reasons. Now I had to worry about George and his brain health. Correction. Now, I had to worry about Sarah taking charge of the man and his brain. I couldn't catch a fucking break this holiday season.

I finished up with Ollie, setting her on the floor to keep herself occupied with some of her toys. "Your turn, Demi."

Freddie stood in his crib, his little hands wrapped around the bars.

Ethan freed him. "She's so mean, your mom."

"Yeah, I'm terrible." I didn't bother saying Freddie was fine. It was good to see Ethan and Fred bond.

"It's good to admit this. Best to get things out into the open, no matter how painful."

"Says the man hiding in the nursery with me to avoid... what? Or who?"

"I'm not avoiding George and his dick comments. I think he's harmless. Mostly."

"He's something. But, no, I was thinking of Lisa." I dove in. "Have you thought about what we discussed in the library?"

"It's hard, ya know. Being the man in the relationship. You and Sarah don't have to worry about—"

"Our fragile male egos?"

He sat in the rocking chair, and I handed off Demi while taking Fred in my arms. "Fredster, your turn."

Freddie cooed.

Ollie chucked a stuffed animal into the back of my legs.

"Sometimes I get images of Olivia in her teen years, and it terrifies me."

"Casey will probably have already graduated from Harvard."

I nodded. "Go on. Before I interrupted you about being the man."

"It's not easy. Not making ends meet. I feel like the answer is simple, but I can't even see the question to know how to get from A to Z."

"Are there expenses you can cut?"

"I've scaled us back to bare bones. Want to adopt our cat? She has expensive urinary tract food. And, you can't really leave her alone much. Our neighbor's daughter is popping in to check on her. For a fee, of course." He groaned.

"Uh, I can ask Sarah." Just what I needed. A high medical needs cat.

"Lisa would kill me. Sometimes I think she loves Minnie more than she loves me."

"Your cat's name is Minnie?" How did I not know this?

"It's short for Wilhelmina." He shrugged.

"Obviously."

"I think I made a huge mistake." His voice was soft, filled with emotion.

Fairly certain he wasn't referring to the cat's name, I said, "Tell me about it."

"I should have gone with her. If her mom dies and I'm here —I don't know how she'll forgive me."

Finished with Freddie, I sat on a quilt on top of the toy chest, with Fred on my lap. "Has there been an update about her mom's status?"

His face darkened, but he didn't answer.

"Not good, then. Well, you have two choices. Leave Casey with us and head out there, or—"

"I don't have the money!"

Demi momentarily stirred in his arms.

I eyed him, understanding this was why he'd followed me for diaper duty. "I'm going to take the kids downstairs and drop them off for Allen and Casey to watch. Then I'm heading to the library to boot up my computer and purchase the next available flight out of Denver. With the storm, it may not be until tomorrow night, but it's better than nothing."

He avoided looking at me. "I can't let you do that."

"I'm not asking for permission, Ethan. I'm letting you know I'm putting your ass on a plane. Consider this my way of saying, you're an effing wet blanket this holiday season and I want you out of my house." With raised hands, I gestured it was useless to argue.

He shrugged one shoulder and casually leaned his head to swipe the dampness from his eyes as if I hadn't noticed his swell of emotion. Proving yet again, men had such fragile egos, even highly-evolved ones like Ethan.

"Can we keep this a secret? I don't want people to actually think you're a good person." He tried laughing, but it turned into a snort.

"Oh, I'm a Petrie. No worries there."

"You should have given your kids Sarah's last name."

"She wouldn't hear of it. I argued until I was blue in the face. For some reason, the woman thinks I have potential." I gestured that was a crazy notion.

"Clearly, she's misinformed."

"Any way you slice it, it's still a hideous name: Petrie." I chuckled. "Come on. I need you to help me so I don't misspell your name or anything. Simple things cause me enormous trouble."

CHAPTER NINE

After purchasing the ticket, we traipsed through the madness of the family room, where the twins sat at the craft table, working on some Christmassy activity given all the red and green, but the concept was beyond me.

"Daddy, we need your help." Casey sat at a black card table with Allen, who was holding Demi on his lap, in front of the fireplace, working on an insanely difficult thousand piece *Finding Dory* jigsaw puzzle I'd purchased for her yesterday on a last-minute trip to the toy store. The puzzle had what seemed like a million Nemos with one Dory in the middle, so the vast majority of the pieces were orange.

"Sure thing, honey." Ethan took a seat at the table, ruffling the top of Casey's head.

Mickey's Christmas Carol played on the television.

"Any progress?" I leaned over her shoulder to inspect.

"Some," Allen said in an *I won't be beat* voice.

"May the puzzle force be with you." I waved goodbye and whizzed through the kitchen to ensure nothing was on fire. Not really knowing what I should look for besides smoke, and not seeing any, I buzzed through into the living room, where I spied Maddie cozying up to Gabe in front of the fireplace. At least that situation was smoothing out for the moment. As much as it could considering both were thinking of popping the question after dating for such a short time. They hadn't even moved in together. Shouldn't that be the first step?

Dad and Helen were with them.

Where were Peter and Tie?

Scratch that. I didn't want to know.

For several blissful moments, no one seemed to notice I was in the room, and I was able to pull up my mental drawbridge and disappear inside my head to my happy place.

"Lizzie, can you help me on the back deck?"

I turned around to see Sarah's red face, an indication she'd just come back inside. "Of course, sweetheart."

In the kitchen, I whispered, "Everything okay?"

Sarah didn't answer, but her expression was deadly serious.

Gandhi zipped by, with Hank right on his tail. "That's my boy," I said.

"The little dog doesn't stand a chance with our cat."

"I'd always bought into the theory dogs chased cats."

"Not in our family." Sarah offered a thin-lipped smile.

Considering the day's events so far, that made perfect sense.

We arrived at the back door. "You ready?" Sarah asked, her hand on the knob.

I was afraid to inquire what I had to prepare for, exactly.

One step outside answered my question when a small clay pot whizzed past my head, landing in a pile of snow. "Whoa!" I scooted Sarah behind me, my arms out to protect her. "No throwing things!"

Tie had one arm behind her head, ready to launch another pot at Peter.

"Tie." I motioned with both hands for her to set the weapon down. "It would be great if we could get through the night without a trip to the emergency room or the neighbors summoning the police."

She didn't let go, nor did she launch it. "He's such an asshole!"

This was a completely different Tie than the one who'd whisked George off to the library. Was this the real Tie behind closed doors?

"I'm an asshole?" Peter covered his chest with a hand. "You're insane and a bitch."

It was Sarah's turn to shout. "Whoa! That language won't be tolerated." She poked a mom-like finger at Peter and then at Tie. "By either of you. It's Christmas Eve for fuck's sake!"

I wasn't sure if I should admonish Sarah for swearing. I didn't think she was offended by all curse words, but certain ones got her feminist hackles up.

Neither of them seemed to notice Sarah's hypocrisy.

"What's going on?" I asked.

"I can't take it anymore." Tie dropped the pot onto the snow below her.

"*You* can't? Try being me!" Peter lunged toward her, but I seized his arm, impeding his progress. "She's a terrible mother!"

Peter, raised by one of the world's worst, would know.

"You're a terrible father!" Tie countered.

My brother hadn't been the best sibling to grow up with, but I didn't think he warranted this charge against his parental skills. Still, I deemed it wise not to get in the middle. More than I already was, given I literally stood between them in an attempt to prevent bloodshed.

"And you're nothing but a cheat! In everything!" Her voiced hurled past howler monkey screech level to something that was completely indescribable.

Sarah and I stared at each other for a moment, neither of us all that keen to press for details. Inside, I could see Maddie and

Gabe at the kitchen table refilling their eggnog glasses. Dad and Helen, each with a twin on one hip, joined them, laughing. Rose now cuddled Demi.

How did they not notice the Peter and Tie brouhaha? The pots were landing in snow and not making much noise, but there was shouting. Of course, the music played in the background, and the wind outside was battering the backside of the house. And Sarah's Christmas display was blinding. Possibly they were determined to stay out of Peter and Tie-phoon's drama at all costs. God knows I wanted to. Years ago, I barely had a relationship with my brother, and I wished that was the case right now. It was difficult for me to muster the energy to care if he had an affair. Or to ferret out if Tie was lying. Maybe it was the historian in me, wanting to see proof of this alleged bun in the oven. Or maybe my old *I don't need the Petries in my life* mantra was rearing its head once again.

"Look," I said in a tone I hoped was soothing. "This really isn't the time for this. For the sake of everyone's holiday, including your daughter's." I jerked my head toward the window and asked, "Is this a conversation you two can table for after Christmas?" I used my *let's be civil* voice.

"That's all we do. Table everything!" Peter raked a hand through his snow-splattered hair, seemingly fighting to control his emotions. "I'm through. Once the holidays are over, I'm talking to my lawyer." He peered around me. "Get yourself a lawyer, *darling*, because mine is going to screw the shit out of you! And good luck trying to prove I have a love-child out there, because it's just not true. This past year with you has been hell, and there isn't enough Viagra in the world to help me get it up!"

That was a nugget about my brother's personal life I didn't need. I didn't think it wise to verbalize the fact he planned to screw her out of everything, but I'd never been on the brink of divorce, so what did I know about how battle lines were drawn?

An odd upward twist of Tie's lips nearly stopped my heart. "Oh, I think I'll be the one screwing the shit out of you, darling."

"Tie, let's go inside." Sarah put an arm around her shoulders and practically dragged the woman inside the house.

Peter kicked a pile of shoveled snow, immediately hopping on one foot, reaching for the other since he'd made direct contact with an ice chunk or possibly the deck railing. "Fuck!" He dragged out the word.

The evening was shaping up to be one for the history books. That was if any of us survived. I thought of Agatha Christie's novel *And Then There Were None*. In the book, though, a killer was picking off people on the island one by one. The rate we were going, some type of family nuclear explosion was moments away, zapping all of us into oblivion.

Peter leaned against the railing and pulled a pack of Marlboros out of his black trousers. He tapped the filter end against the cardboard box before placing it in his mouth and used a monogrammed Zippo lighter to ignite it. With the cigarette between his reddened lips due to the cold, he asked, "You want one?"

"Nope. Those things will kill you." Just ask Lisa's mom.

"The sooner the better." He inhaled deeply, looking skyward as if willing God to strike him dead. He sighed and then asked, "Have you ever had one before, Miss Goodie Two-Shoes? As your big brother, it's my job to try to corrupt you."

I snorted. "Now that we're both grown and with children, you want to be my big brother? Timing isn't your thing, apparently."

He shrugged. "It's amazing when you think of it. How old we are. How in the fuck did I become middle-aged? With that *thing* as my wife?" He flicked his fingers, the cigarette between them, toward the house, where we could see Tie talking with Maddie and Gabe. It was as if the fight moments earlier hadn't left an impression on Tie whatsoever, considering she was laughing and looked completely at ease.

It sent chills down my spine.

"What's going on, Peter?"

"She's impossible. Insane. Vindictive." His cigarette hand mimed the list of negatives was endless, the red tip singeing a snowflake.

"Just like Mom." I rubbed my hands together and tucked my head into the high collar of my cardigan to protect myself from another blast of wind kicking up. Unlike Peter, I didn't have a winter jacket on, and the temperature seemed to drop one degree per second.

He bobbed his head but didn't speak for several seconds. He blew out a plume of smoke and coughed a little. "I'm sorry. She wasn't nice to you, and…" He shifted on his feet. "Neither was I."

Taken aback, I stared at Snoopy's doghouse, one of the lights flickering as if about to flame out.

He took another drag. "You're a good person, Elizabeth. Always have been. I hope…" He looked up from the snow and leveled his eyes on mine. "I hope we can be friends at least. God knows I can use one right now."

"O-of course." I couldn't think of what I should say or do. What would Sarah do? "Should we hug it out or something?" I let out a nervous bark of laughter. "That's what Sarah would advise."

He pulled me into an embrace, stepping on my right foot as I stumbled into his chest. "You're lucky to have her. She's brought out the best in you."

Stunned, I remained quiet until we separated from the awkward hug, the first I could remember. "Does this truce mean you're going to stop trying to steal my inheritance from Dad? I have twins, you know," I said in a teasing voice.

"Can't. Promised Mom on her death bed I'd screw you out of everything." His smile was genuine, but it cut to the bone.

"If you're counting on outing me to Dad on his deathbed, news flash, he knows I'm a lesbian. You won't be able to pull another Uncle Jerry." I slugged his arm in lame sibling fashion.

Peter turned whiter than the falling snow. "Y-you know about that?"

I nodded. "Mom gloated about it to my face."

He turned his head so I couldn't see his expression. "Does Dad know?" His voice was barely audible.

"Yes. I told him recently."

"I—" He covered his mouth with his hand, his fingers bright red and the knuckles ghostly white. "I don't know what to say."

"Just tell me one thing. Did you come up with the idea yourself, or was it Mom?"

Peter nodded, seeming to understand why I asked. Another gust of wind caused the falling snow to splatter both of our faces. In the midst of the turmoil, he said, "It was me, but she encouraged me once I shared my plan."

The back of my throat burned. "Thanks." He appeared puzzled, so I clarified, "Not for the dirty rotten trick but for being honest. It helps in a bizarre way. I can't explain it." I swallowed. "I think we should get back inside."

"I need a second." He walked to the far end of the deck, the snow crunching underfoot, making me wince as if he was dragging his nails down a chalkboard. At the top of the stairs, he stopped and crossed his arms, keeping his back to me. I couldn't tell if he was crying, but his shoulders shuddered some. More than likely it was due to the weather.

Inside the house, I shook off the snow, mostly on the mat but a few drops of water sprinkled onto the hardwood floor.

Sarah mouthed, "Everything okay?"

I stared at her, wondering if everything was. I should be pissed. Beyond pissed. But the only emotion swirling inside me was emptiness mixed with an odd sense of relief to have finally confronted Peter about something.

All smiles, Sarah excused herself from Rose and Troy, who now held the twinks in the typical *hand-off the twins* fashion that happened when everyone gathered, and beelined for me. She steered us to the small powder room off the family room. "The library is taken by Maddie, Gabe, and Ethan," she explained to my unspoken question. "He's talking about heading out to see Lisa tomorrow. His fears."

I nodded, unsure if Sarah was aware we paid for his last-minute flight, which wasn't cheap. Not that she would give a flying fuck about the cost.

"What happened?" The concern on Sarah's face increased fivefold.

"A lot." I scratched the top of my head. "But nothing new."

Her brow furrowed, and I could tell she was trying to be patient but also cognizant that we had a household full of guests on Christmas Eve. "Can you give me a clue? Is there any truth about—?"

Before she could bring up Tie's accusation, which for some reason I couldn't let infiltrate my mind tonight, I interjected, "Uncle Jerry." I tucked my hands into my armpits to combat the burning tingling sensation now that I was out of the cold.

"Your mom's brother?"

I confirmed with a nod. "Peter did it. On his own."

"Wh-what—?" Her dark brown eyes tinged with understanding, making them even darker, not to mention alluring in a smoldering way.

Was that wrong? To find her insanely beautiful at this particular moment?

"How did that come up?" she asked.

I coughed into my shoulder, followed by a sniffle. *No, Lizzie, this isn't the time to get sick, even if you wanted to earlier. Your family needs you to hold everything together.* "Um, that's a good question." I replayed snippets of the conversation in my head. "He tried to get me to smoke, saying it was his big brotherly duty to corrupt me. I countered he was late to the sibling game. That led us to Peter acknowledging Mom wasn't nice to me and he wasn't either." I closed my eyes to zero in on the crucial piece. "Then, I asked if he'd stop trying to steal my inheritance, and I ended up joking he wouldn't be able to pull an Uncle Jerry with Dad since he knew I was gay. That's how I ended up here." I motioned to the powder room, with a tiny Christmas tree on the counter with battery-operated red and green lights. "Oh, he also mentioned you bring out the best in me."

Sarah sized me up. She'd been trying to get me to open up more, especially with my father and brother. I was 99.78 percent sure she hadn't meant for me to do it on Christmas Eve when this particular evening was already brimming on exploding into a shitstorm.

But, I'd learned in therapy, things surfaced when you least expected them to.

"Wow," she said.

"I'm sorry." I rested my forehead on her shoulder. "You've worked so hard to make this day special, and everyone, including me, is intent on ruining it."

She wrapped her arms around me. "It's okay. I've learned to roll with the punches with this family."

I pulled back. "I need to talk to Dad. Peter asked if he knew and—that upset him the most." I reached for the doorknob. Over my shoulder, I asked, "How's Tie?"

"Calm." Sarah's expression confirmed a calm Tie was more dangerous than an angry one. "I think she got the outcome she wanted out of Peter tonight. Now all of us have to wait and see what she intends to do with everything. I don't trust her one bit. Nor do I trust Peter."

I kissed Sarah's cheek and left in search of my father in the living room.

He held Demi, who was sound asleep.

"Hey there." I brushed the hair off Demi's forehead, careful not to wake her. "Her crib is set up. Shall we take her upstairs to let her sleep?"

"Are you okay?" He peered at me with his unusually perceptive eyes.

"Did Peter talk to you?"

Without another word, he made way for the staircase, with me in tow.

It didn't take long to settle Demi, snuggling peacefully on top of the soft sheet with baby elephants.

Outside the nursery, I motioned for Dad to enter a spare bedroom at the top of the stairs. He took a seat in the charcoal gray microfiber chair.

I perched on the edge of the bed, crossing my arms.

Dad didn't speak.

Staring at a montage of small framed black and white photos on the wall above his head, I said, "I wanted to give you the heads-up about Peter." I queried his face, trying to determine if I was too late. Unable to decipher his poker-face, I asked, "Has he talked to you in the last ten minutes?"

Dad shook his head.

"I told him I knew about Uncle Jerry—how he outed me for my portion of the inheritance."

"I see." His face remained stoic, but his shoulders slumped a smidge.

"He knows that you know. Peter asked, and I didn't want to—"

Dad nodded. "You did the right thing. There's been enough intrigue and lying." He slanted his head. "Are you okay?"

I retightened my ponytail to the point where all the hair was almost painfully constricted. "I really don't know. This night hasn't gone according to plan."

Right then, Sarah hollered loud enough for those in the North Pole to hear, "Okay, everyone. Get your jackets. We're going caroling in five minutes."

A hint of a smile appeared on Dad's face. "I'll stay with Demi. Can you tell Peter to join me?"

In the entryway, I spied Peter huddling by the umbrella stand, trying his best to blend into the surroundings so his wife wouldn't see him. All those years, it had been me hiding. I sidled up next to him and whispered Dad was in the guest room and wanted to speak to him. He trudged up the stairs, looking like a child on his way to receive a whipping.

Sarah noticed, but she had her *everything's jolly* smile firmly in place. "I'll get the twins ready." She led them upstairs, their chubby legs slowly taking one step at a time. Given it was Christmas Eve, their usual bedtime had been thrown out the window.

Maddie slipped next to me and whispered in my ear, "Sarah's insane. The storm is really kicking up."

I shrugged. "Caroling is on the schedule for seven sharp, followed by dinner at eight fifteen, after putting the twins down for bed at eight."

Pulling on his jacket, Ethan asked, "How many air mattresses do you own? I got an alert that I-25 may close."

My neck nearly snapped when I whipped around to look out the open front door. "Are you telling me everyone who doesn't live in Fort Collins may have to stay the night?" My mind tallied potential overnight guests, but I couldn't get past two names and the implication of waking up on Christmas morning with Peter and Tie. That was if one didn't kill the other in the middle of the night. How would I explain that to detectives? *Well, we knew it was possible, but the roads were closed so we locked them in the basement together, hoping none of us would get caught in the crosshairs.*

I fucking hated Christmas with my family!

"Gabe doesn't think we should try to drive to my apartment. And my parents flight for early tomorrow has already been cancelled. They're hoping to arrive on the twenty-sixth for our week in Vail." Maddie gave me her *aren't you thrilled Sarah planned this party* sarcastic smirk.

Ethan checked his phone. "My flight is still on."

"It's later in the day. I'm sure it'll be fine," Maddie assured him.

My mind could only focus on the house guests currently under my roof. "Okay. Rose and Troy are only a few blocks away. They can walk home," I said in hopes that would be the case hours from now.

"Lizzie!" Ethan and Maddie screeched, more for effect than concern.

Ignoring them, I started to concoct a plan to have Tie stay with Rose. Should I ship Ethan and Peter to George's across the street? Or would that snowball into the two starting a divorce club?

"Do we really have to go caroling?" Casey whined. "It's so cold out." She exaggerated a shiver and fell into my legs.

I hunched down. "We don't have a lot of time. What do you want?"

"Are you bribing me?" Her eyes grew three sizes.

"Absolutely."

She bit the tip of her index finger. "I have been wanting a microscope."

"Done!" I stuck out my hand, which she shook.

Ethan said, "I think I'll stay behind and ensure the turkey doesn't catch fire."

Casey waved for her father to bend over, and she whispered in his ear.

Ethan turned to me with keen interest. "I hear—"

I stabbed the air with a palm. "Spit it out. I have a few more people to take care of before Sarah returns. Casey, are you taking notes of all the promises? God knows my mind is spent."

She tapped the side of her head. "Gotcha covered."

"The Harry Potter books," Ethan blurted.

I widened my eyes. "Wasn't expecting that, but okay."

Casey nudged my leg. "He's asking for me."

Tie bustled closer, shrugging her coat on. "This is fun. Isn't this fun? I need to use the bathroom before we head out."

Casey and I smiled as if in tune. Not having to bribe Tie was a victory.

Maddie was a different matter. Tapping her fingertips together, she said in a mafioso-like voice, "I hear you're the one I need to talk to."

I shook a fist at Ethan. "What?" I asked Maddie.

"A panorama lens for my camera."

I glanced down at Casey, and she indicated Maddie's request was seared into her memory bank.

Gabe and Allen stood behind Maddie.

"Really, my own brothers?" I groaned.

"Broncos tickets," Gabe said without an ounce of chagrin. "Any game."

"The latest book on the Russian Revolution," Allen said in all seriousness.

"Okay, Dad and Peter are staying. Who's next?"

Helen raised her hand. "A massage."

Rose chimed in, "I choose that as well." She turned to Helen. "We should go together. With Sarah."

George, with a blank face but in a keen voice said, "A new dog bed for Gandhi."

I sighed. Funny, when he needed to be, he was completely lucid. "Okay, Troy, you're the last one. Your demand?"

Troy stroked his chin. "I don't really mind going out and singing. I think it's a nice thing to do on Christmas Eve."

"You hear that, everyone? Troy is the only decent family member. The rest of you, I've got your number." I circled my index finger in the air.

"Not scared of you, Lizzie. Ever." Maddie leaned into Gabe's chest.

"What did I miss?" Tie asked, straightening her jacket. I wouldn't put it past the woman to steal anything and everything from the powder room.

"N-nothing," I stammered, relieved no one had filled her in.

Sarah descended the stairs with the twins bundled into puffy navy-blue snowsuits. "What's going on?"

"We're all super excited to sing our hearts out," I said with too much exuberance, but Sarah was busy making sure Ollie didn't trip Fred on the stairs and didn't catch my mistake.

"Lizzie, will you lead the way? I'll bring up the rear." Sarah gave me her *don't argue* glare.

"Follow me, merry carolers." I led the motley crew to the first victims', I mean neighbors' house.

After the group gathered in the entryway and walked to Betty's house, the neighbor who'd considered me insane after I threatened to murder Gandhi— George's dog not the Indian leader who was already dead—I rang the bell.

Ralph, her husband, answered.

Sarah burst into "Jingle Bells," the rest of us joining in out of fear for our lives. At least, that was my motivation. Since I considered it was cruel and unusual punishment for anyone to hear me sing, I mouthed the words.

Ralph and Betty, with their arms laced around each other's waist, grinned and swayed to the music. When we finished, Betty said, "That was lovely. Thank you." Her smile turned into a grimace when her eyes swept mine, but she adjusted when blocking me from her sight. "I feel like we should reward you.

Hold on." She dashed inside, returning with a fruitcake loaf. She thrust it at me.

It weighed a ton, and I wondered if she'd planned to take me out with it all along. "Uh, thanks. We'll put this to good use." I envisioned knocking some heads if anyone got out of line later.

"At nine sharp, we're having champagne if you want to join us," Sarah said, rallying the troops to move to the next house.

Was she going to invite the whole fricking neighborhood for champagne? How many bottles did we have in the basement fridge? Had she planned this all along? Should I be this upset for Sarah's jolliness?

No, I shouldn't. Clearly.

The next house was a neighbor I didn't know, meaning I hadn't offended or shocked them in any way. That I knew of.

Maddie, maybe in tune with my sour mood, took over the doorbell ringing duty. This house had the honor of hearing one of my favorite Christmas tunes, "Little Drummer Boy."

While it was one of my faves, it quickly became apparent I didn't know the words and I wasn't in the minority. Most of us consulted the music sheets Sarah had provided, each encased in protective plastic. She really had prepared for every eventuality, including caroling into what was quickly reaching blizzard conditions.

Much to my surprise, Ethan not only knew all the words, but with his soulful voice, eyes closed, and one hand holding Casey's tightly, he was moving to watch. The rest of us stuck with "Pa rum pum pum pum" while he did the heavy lifting.

Once again, Sarah invited the man and woman, whose names I hadn't caught, for champagne. This time, Maddie quirked a brow at me. Okay, if Maddie thought it insane to invite every Tom, Dick, and Harry to the party, maybe I wasn't irked for all the wrong reasons.

Before we reached the final house at the end of the street, I looped my arm through Sarah's and whispered in her ear, "What are you doing?"

"Caroling." Her voice was shaky at best.

"And inviting everyone for champagne. Why?" I practically had my mouth pressed to her ear.

Sarah sucked in a deep breath. "It's Christmas."

"Not buying that," I said through a smile since Allen and Gabe turned around to see if we'd overheard a joke they'd cracked since both men were laughing. "And most neighbors are with their own families."

Sarah broke free from my grasp and led the group to the next house, forcing me to hoof it to match her stride.

"What's going on? Really?" I asked. "Why are you inviting the world back to the house?"

"Please, I've only invited a few people. Not the world."

"Talk to me. I know this wasn't on the schedule." I gambled it wasn't.

Through gritted teeth, she said, "Because nothing is going right tonight. I'm hoping if more people come, it'll stall whatever's brewing next for the worst Petrie Christmas in history." Sarah rested her head against mine.

Her plan wasn't all that bad if the Petries were your typical family. And adding Tie into the mix was potentially the spark that'd ignite the powder keg, destroying everyone in her wake.

"Do I need to make a champagne run?" I asked in an effort to show my support. Conjuring a way to get the car out of the driveway was a concern.

Sarah gave my cheek a quick peck. "Got it covered."

Of course, she did.

I nodded, understanding her thoughts. "What can I do, Sarah?"

"Kill Tie or Peter. I'll let you take your pick."

"I was hoping you wouldn't start with capital murder."

"Does Colorado have the death penalty?" she asked in a rational voice.

"I'm pretty sure it does."

"Oh, well, don't do that, then."

We reached the house before I could figure out if her murder request had been sincere.

Even in jest, it made one thing absolutely clear. Tie and Peter were a disease. If not treated soon, they'd kill us all. Not literally. At least, I didn't think so. The earlier basement scenario played in my head again. Maybe that was the solution. Lock them up and see who survived.

Sarah rang the bell, and the occupants of the blue house spilled outside to a rousing version of "I Saw Mommy Kissing Santa Claus," and the way we were heading, this was a real possibility. However, given my father had been roped into dressing like Santa Claus later to hand out early gifts, the thought made my head spin contemplating the future therapy bills.

I faded into the back of the group to keep an eye on Tie and to come up with a plan. What, though? She wasn't the type to scare easily, and I had zero dirt on her. *You know it's bad, Lizzie, when you're thinking of ways to blackmail your sister-in-law on Christmas.*

Maddie.

She could help me formulate a plan.

I inched closer to my favorite shit-stirrer and tugged on the hem of her puffy jacket.

Confused, she swiveled her neck and mouthed, "What?"

I motioned with my head, indicating I wanted a private consultation.

She mouthed, "Now?"

I repeated the motion with more force.

She rolled her eyes.

As the group launched into the chorus, I said to Maddie,

"Tie. You need to help me take her out. Not literally, but... you know."

"Just how in the world do you think we can do that without it blowing up in our faces? Tie isn't stupid. And she's meaner than a rabid dog."

"There has to be a way. That's why Sarah's inviting everyone over. To stop Tie from whatever the hell she's planning." I had a decent idea of what her plot entailed. A pregnancy bombshell, but I didn't know how she planned to deliver it. Parachute in a pregnant lady as everyone opened their gifts on Christmas morning? Would she do that to her daughter, though? Or was she banking on Demi being too young to remember? What about my children? They were also young, but I didn't want them around this type of behavior. Not at all.

Maddie's head bobbed up and down. "That makes sense. I was starting to think being married to you had completely warped Sarah's mind."

I put a gloved finger on my nose and then pointed at her. "That. I need you to do more of that but not directed at me. Take her out, Maddie."

"*Carte blanche?*"

"As long as no one gets arrested or maimed, yes. Do your worst or best."

Maddie knitted her brow. "Do I have a deadline?"

"Uh, tonight, but that might be asking too much, even for you."

The carolers finished, and we walked ahead of them in order not to be overheard.

I put a hand on Maddie's shoulder and whispered, "It's up to you, Mads. Don't let Sarah down."

"Seriously, Lizzie. You need to work on your dramatic flair."

"Stop wasting time on me!" I whispered harshly in her ear.

Maddie started to roll her eyes, but they clouded over. "I

wish I had more time to prepare. Taking down the likes of Tie isn't a simple matter."

"Oh, please. You've been wanting to do this since you found out she was Peter's mistress."

"Wanting and doing are two different things. And I haven't given her much thought in months, really."

We trudged through the thickening snow on the way back to our house.

Gabe, Allen, and Ethan had their arms locked, walking in exaggerated goose step fashion, belting out "Santa Claus is Coming to Town."

It seemed Sarah's caroling plan had accomplished one goal at least; it was hard to feel Scrooge-like when spreading Christmas cheer with friends.

Tie inserted herself between Maddie and me, looping an arm through each of ours. "Isn't this a magical night?"

"That's one way of looking at it," Maddie said.

"Maybe there'll be a Christmas miracle or two," Tie continued. "Wouldn't you like that, Maddie?"

"Do you have a miracle in mind?" Maddie responded.

"Oh, I don't have control of these things, but I do think things will change so you can be reunited with someone from your past."

Was she going to announce her impending separation from Peter at dinner, releasing my brother from his miserable marriage to allow him to chase the girl that got away: Maddie? As far as I knew, Sarah and I were the only ones aware of Peter's threat about hiring a divorce lawyer. The frost between them, though, wasn't difficult to decipher.

How would Tie's professed miracle impact my stepbrother's plan to ask Maddie, Peter's ex, to marry him?

If this were a movie, viewers would think it unrealistic.

But this was my life.

For better or worse.

CHAPTER TEN

While I was heading back downstairs after tucking in the twinks, a cowbell rang, and Maddie announced in a booming voice, "Dinner is served!"

Sarah's frosty glare made it crystal clear to me Maddie had improvised her announcement duties. Never ask a practical joker/interior designer, who's latest project was a palatial ranch for a cowboy tycoon, to take her announcement duties seriously. The guests seemed to appreciate the effort, including Tie. Would it fit over her head so all of us could take a turn gonging the bell? Was this step one in Maddie's destroy Tie plan? Torture by cowbell? That might be hard to prove in court? Premeditated cowbell?

To avoid potential conflict at the dinner table, Sarah and Maddie had devised a seating chart. At each place was one of the pinecone things I'd made and the person's name, although with Lisa's absence, we had an extra space. Sarah had the presence of mind to remove the pinecone and chair, leaving a gap between Peter and the person to his right.

Much to my dismay, I was wedged between Tie and Ethan. Had they thought this one through, considering Ethan's marriage woes and Peter's earlier threat? Even if the threat had been uttered after the chart had been finalized, we all had a stake in the *when will Peter divorce Tie* bet.

Allen, Troy, and Ethan had been enlisted as servers by Sarah weeks ago, and each wore a red apron stating *Christmas calories don't count*. Did that go for marriage woes, threats, or whatnot? Gabe wore an elf hat and a gray so-called man apron, an early Christmas gift from Maddie, that had pockets for a phone, ketchup, mustard, beer, and matches according to the sketches on the fabric. Since ketchup, mustard, and matches weren't needed for this evening's soiree, he filled those pockets with candy canes, presumably for those who finished their meals. A still-capped New Belgium Accumulation, a winter white IPA, resided in the beer pocket. He plunked the twenty-pound turkey at the end of the table.

The servers, also in elf hats, arranged the side dishes in the center of the table, offering mashed potatoes, glazed carrots, cranberry sauce, parsnips, sausage stuffing, green bean casserole, and candied yams.

"Just for you, Lizzie." Ethan placed piping hot macaroni and cheese in front of me.

"You shouldn't have," I joked.

"I didn't. Your wife did." Ethan took his seat on my left, not bothering to take off his apron or hat.

I glanced at Sarah, once again reminded how much effort she'd put into everything.

"Do you intend to share?" asked Allen, right across from me, with Casey on his right.

"Only to those who behave." I made my voice a smidge too threatening, causing Allen to gulp. I waggled my brows to put him at ease, but my charm had the opposite effect.

Fortunately, Gabe fired up the electric knife, getting down to business and nullifying conversations for a brief respite. The decision about who should carve the turkey had been a no-brainer to me, although Maddie and Sarah had gone back and forth on it. Dad was useless when it came to matters like this, a fact he owned. Arming Peter seemed much too dangerous, and I'd thought that before the scene on the back deck. I had no intentions of cutting up a bird. Nor did Sarah or Maddie.

Gabe seemed to take a short break but kept the blade going. Had Sarah or Maddie given him a look to take meticulous care when carving to keep the racket up for as long as possible? What was next? Blasting Christmas music over the speakers? Was Alexa smart enough to pick up verbal clues to drown out dinner-party spats?

Peter, on the other side as far away from Tie as possible, looked shell-shocked. Every time Gabe sliced another piece of white meat, Peter turned a shade greener.

The process of dishing out sides began in earnest, and I passed Ethan the mac and cheese after serving myself a healthy portion.

Some initiated table talk to those sitting next to them, and the only ones who looked as if they were enjoying themselves were Rose, Troy, and George. Gandhi circled the table, his tail wagging. Hank was nowhere in sight. Leave it to the prey animal to know when to scram.

Ethan nudged my side for me to accept the green bean casserole from Allen. I handed it off without scooping any on my plate, but I did steal a crispy French's fried onion in the process.

"Cheater," he said, sounding like a 1920s' gangster.

"Are you going to make me swim with the fishes?" I scooped parsnips, one of the few veggies I'd eat, onto my plate and handed the dish to Allen, who regarded it suspiciously before taking a tiny serving and then holding the platter for Casey.

"Perhaps. Or torture you." Ethan plopped mashed potatoes onto his plate.

Casey eyed my parsnip portion and matched it.

Sarah cleared her throat. Had she overheard the mafia conversation and wanted to nip it in the bud before giving the reprehensible guests certain ideas? She rose to her feet, holding a wineglass. "I want to thank all of you for coming tonight and making this holiday special." Her smile, even to a casual observer, was forced.

Feeling compelled to add to her sentiment, I got to my feet, clutching my crystal water glass filled with Perrier. "Yes, thank you for coming out on such an awful night—I mean, weather-wise." Unsure where to go from there but wanting to issue a clear directive that no one should do anything else to unravel all of Sarah's hard work, I raised my glass and said, "To my beautiful wife, who slaved away for weeks to make this evening special." My eyes swept all of the guests before I took a sip.

There were several *hear, hears*, and the group tucked into their meals with gusto. It didn't take long for a sprinkling of conversation and laughter to trickle throughout the room.

Tie leaned forward to lure Ethan into whatever trap she had opted for. "What are you going to do about your marriage?" She stage-whispered the last word, and I could only hope she did so since Casey was seated across from us.

Ethan's eyes darted to his young daughter, who was more perceptive than most adults walking the earth, and didn't take the bait, pretending not to hear Tie. Casey, much to my relief, didn't react to the question. Or was she acting?

"Allen, how are your Russian lessons coming along?" I spoke in a commanding voice to steer the conversation to something safer.

Allen covered his mouth to avoid spraying food and spoke around a bite, "They're fun. The tutor you found is quite the character, but it's not an easy language to master. The tricky part is getting accustomed to the grammar structure." He visibly swallowed, pressing a palm onto his chest to aid the process. "Once I master the alphabet, it'll be easier to pronounce the words. They say words like they're spelled. Also, their sentence structure is simpler. For example, in English, I'd say, 'Lizzie, can you please pass me the parsnips?' While they'd say, 'Give parsnips please.'"

I nodded. "It takes some getting used to. Being so direct."

"And the parsnips?" Allen's eyes fell to the plate that had found its way back to me.

"Oh!" I passed him the tray. "My apologies. I thought you were simply edifying."

"Killing two birds with one stone." He smiled.

"Give mac and cheese." Casey waited several seconds before adding the word please.

Ethan rolled his eyes. "Thanks for that, Allen. I have a feeling that's going to stick."

Allen stood to reach the mac and cheese dish and held it for Casey. After setting it back, Allen retook his seat and said to Ethan, "You know, Casey would excel with foreign languages. Does her school have a program?"

"Nope," Ethan said a little gruffly.

Was he angry with Allen for planting the seed in Casey's brain or with his inability to pay for private lessons? With the Internet, finding videos wouldn't be all that hard. That probably wasn't the issue, though. It was yet another reminder of how strained his finances were and the challenge of providing for an off-the-charts intelligent child who was more than likely bored with her public-school education. I wouldn't be surprised, given the right support, if she'd graduate high school in her early teens and head off to the likes of Harvard before she could drive.

"Anton, my tutor, is moving to Fort Collins, so I'll be coming up here once a week. She can join my lessons." Allen met my eyes as if it just struck him that he shouldn't have said anything before consulting me since I was paying for said lessons.

To put Allen at ease and to cut off Ethan's gut reaction to say no to gifts or any type of assistance, I said, "That's a great idea. I'll speak to Anton."

I had zero issues paying an extra fee to help Casey get a leg up.

Casey hopped to her feet and raced to Ethan. Seizing his hand and yanking his arm up and down like an old-fashioned water pump, she pleaded with imploring eyes, "Can I, Daddy?"

Ethan knew he was licked. "As long as you behave, and please, don't learn any curse words. Your mother wouldn't be pleased."

"How would she know?" Tie speared a carrot with her fork.

"She has a way of knowing everything." Ethan patted the top of Casey's head.

She stole a cheddar-topped roll off Ethan's plate and headed back to her side of the table.

Again, I roped Allen into my efforts of shoving Tie out of all dinner conversation. "Will your visits coincide with dates with a certain nanny I know?" I sipped my Perrier. Bailey, our nanny, had gone to her grandmother's in California for winter break, and I suspected Allen missed her more than he cared to admit.

Allen's cheeks tinged. "Perhaps."

Next time, Lizzie, don't ask a question that will embarrass him.

Miraculously, Tie picked up on this thread. "Ooooh. Are you dating Lizzie's nanny?"

Surely, she'd known this. Allen and Bailey had been at Thanksgiving, and it was apparent to all they were dating. Quite possibly she thought the situation would get under my skin. Did she think I was so much like my cheating brother and had my sights on Bailey? Was that why she'd gone on earlier about Petries being dawgs? But that didn't make sense, since I clearly didn't show any animus just now. Or was Peter fucking Demi's nanny? Was he that much of a cheater's stereotype?

There was a lull in the dinner conversation, and the effect of being around so many potential bombshells had taken a toll on me. Exhausted, I let my guard down and concentrated on eating.

This turned out to be a mistake.

A terrible one.

George, perhaps feeling pressure to fill the void, announced yet again, "I love dick."

Seriously?

Couldn't the man have had a different phrase on some weird loop in his head? "Cheerios are the best," or something like that?

Casey asked, "Is that—?"

"The TV show starring Kevin Bacon, yes." Sarah set her wineglass down. "Does anyone need more turkey? Let's not let this beautiful bird go to waste."

"Who's Kevin Bacon? His name conjures up some tasty images." George's smile was oddly intimidating.

"You don't know the actor in the show you like?" Casey asked, squinting one eye. I wondered if Ethan ever missed Casey's newborn days, when he still had a chance of being one step ahead of his daughter.

"He looks different in the show." Sarah handed the turkey platter to Peter, who still hadn't touched his plate, but he obligingly added another slice onto his pile.

Tie piped up, "Do you know who else likes dick—the TV show?"

"Give parsnips!" I blurted.

Maddie grabbed the plate and stood to hand it across the table, briefly blocking George from Tie's view. "Lizzie is just mad about parsnips."

George eyed the platter. "They look like shriveled—"

"Weeds," I said. "Tasty weeds. I could live on them."

George's mouth opened, but Ethan beat him to it. "Charades. We should play charades. After dinner, that is. Not now."

Maddie retook her seat. "I love charades."

I didn't, but it didn't seem like the right time to point that out.

"Casey, what did you ask Santa to bring you?" Gabe asked, clearly wanting to do his part to keep the conversation away from dicks.

Honestly, never in a million years did I foresee a Christmas like this one.

With her fork loaded with mashed potatoes, Casey stared at Gabe a tick longer than normal. "Do you believe in Santa?"

Gabe flinched as if not knowing how to respond. Yes, so not to burst her bubble or no and potentially look a fool in front of the brainiac? He opted for yes.

"Me too. The kids at school tried to tell me otherwise, but why would my parents lie to me?"

Ethan swallowed, his eyes on his plate as he scooted mashed taters to scoop up a pool of gravy.

"I know he wasn't really here earlier." She eyed my father, who'd gotten into costume while we caroled to hand out gifts to the little ones, including Casey, before putting the twins to bed.

Tie leaned forward and latched onto the part I feared. "Oh, people lie all the time. Isn't that right, Peter?"

Peter, much to my surprise, refused to take the bait. Instead, he shoved half a slice of turkey into his mouth, the first morsel he'd eaten.

"It's not right to lie," Casey said matter-of-factly. "Is it, Daddy?"

"I think Lizzie has studied that. From a historical perspective, that is, and she could educate us all." Ethan's face had grown whiter.

"Lying is a theme in history, yes."

"As well as adultery," Tie pitched in.

"So, charades. I'm really looking forward to that. I can't remember the last time I played." I cleared my throat and tugged on the collar of my button-up.

"Have you played?" Maddie asked.

I paused and then shrugged. "I'll still kick your—buttocks."

"Does Kevin Bacon have tight buttocks?" George asked.

"What kind of flower is that?" I pointed at the display on the table in hopes Helen would take pity on me.

"The red one?" When I nodded, she continued, "Amaryllis. You have to force them to bloom in time for Christmas." She continued to discuss the steps of prepping the bulb, and I was entirely certain none of us was listening, just relieved that neither George nor Tie pounced on the word *force*.

When she finished, George let out a rip-roaring burp, but no one dared laugh or say a thing. I wondered if someone had preemptively whacked Tie in the shins.

I sought sanctuary in the recesses of my mind, dreaming of a beach holiday for next Christmas. Sarah. The twins. Blue sky. Warm weather. No other fucking Petrie in sight, aside from my wife and offspring. That was the definition of the perfect Christmas.

My eyes wandered to my stunning wife, who was chatting with Maddie and Rose. I didn't think it possible for me to love Sarah more, but each day, our bond only deepened.

While Tie quizzed Allen about Bailey, Ethan bumped my arm and showed me a text from Lisa simply stating: *Merry Christmas.*

I bobbed my head and whispered, "It's a good sign. She must miss you two terribly."

"As do I," he said with honesty.

"Does she know you're arriving tomorrow night?"

He shook his head. "Her uncle is picking me up. Fingers crossed they don't cancel my flight."

"They won't." I wished I could see her eyes when Ethan showed up.

"Lizzie, would you kill your baby brother if he knocked up your nanny?" Tie asked, gripping her wineglass like she wanted to snap the stem in two.

I was in mid-swallow and nearly choked. "What?" I gulped my water, the carbonation burning all the way down. I tapped my chest with a hand to force the remaining bites of parsnips down the wrong pipe. "Why would you ask that?" I looked to Allen. "That's not a possibility, right?" Bailey's grandmother, who'd asked me to look after Bailey, would kill me.

Allen, ashen faced and mute, only managed to gape at Tie's supposition.

"Allen?" I prodded.

He shook his head in such a terrified way I was fairly certain he was still a virgin.

Dad, who'd been conversing with George, eyed Allen but opted not to enter the fray.

"Well, if he did, it's only fitting for the Petrie men. Knocking up women they aren't married to."

Dad shifted in his seat, his eyes aflame.

Helen glared at Tie's profile.

Gabe's stare contained even more menace.

Sarah rested her forehead on her fingertips, stroking her brow.

I queried Peter's stony expression to determine if there was an inkling of truth in Tie's accusation. Was there another child of his somewhere unbeknownst to all of us? Had he fallen in love with someone else and Tie suspected? When she'd mentioned it earlier, I was convinced it was Tie being Tie. But, her harping on the topic and Peter's difficulty with fidelity… Was there a kernel of truth?

"A little bird told me you two are planning to have another baby?" Tie held her wineglass in one hand as if it were a treasure.

My eyes scanned the guests to ferret out the culprit who'd shared this tidbit.

None of the faces registered guilt, although with this family, that meant nothing. This holiday proved I was surrounded by vipers.

"We are." Despite the fact Sarah wasn't thrilled with Tie, she couldn't keep the glee from her eyes, drawing a smile to my face.

"We are," I agreed, staring in Sarah's eyes.

"That calls for a toast." Dad rose to his feet, shocking the hell out of me. "To my beautiful daughter, her lovely wife, and their wonderful family. May the future bring you everything you desire and much more."

"Whoop!" Gabe pounded the table with one palm, raising his beer to his lips with the other.

"Are you going to give it a boy or girl name this time?" Casey asked, clearly still unimpressed by our desire not to allow Olivia and Freddie to wear blue and pink even though we gave them gendered names. The kid never forgot anything. "Although, I know a boy named Oliver who goes by Ollie," she conceded.

"That's a good question," I said. We had talked of names briefly in the past, but it seemed premature to announce a name before we fell pregnant. "Do you have any suggestions?"

"Casey is a good name," she said without a hint of irony. "Works for a boy or girl."

"We'll keep that in mind."

"Are you using your eggs again?" Helen asked.

It wasn't an extremely odd question, given the process involved two women and a sperm donor, but it was difficult to dislodge the knowledge we were eating Christmas Eve dinner and discussing whose eggs we intended to use. I prayed no one asked if we planned to use a turkey baster. The same one we'd used for tonight's meal. We weren't. At least, I didn't think that was part of the plan.

"Mine, this time." Sarah smiled at her mom, who grinned back.

"Does Lizzie not have enough?" Tie asked. "Or do you want to break the Petrie curse?"

No one spoke, but all eyes darted to Tie, who grinned like the Cheshire cat.

"Kidding, of course," she said in a way that conveyed the exact opposite. She opened her mouth but was cut off.

"Is everyone ready for pie?" Helen asked, already rising from her seat.

Rose stood. "I'll help you."

Then Maddie fled, making me think she wasn't up to the task I'd set for her during caroling. But who would be, considering how intent Tie was on destroying the evening? The woman had zero shame. And, Peter. I hadn't wrapped my brain around whether or not I believed he was innocent.

Even Sarah left the table.

"I could use a smoke," Ethan said. "Peter?"

They departed.

Dad and I exchanged a worried look, but I had to wonder what thoughts ran through his head. How was he handling Tie's accusations given the Helen and Allen situation? Challenging Peter was a calculated risk, and maybe this would be part of her divorce lawyer's attack. Taking on Charles Allen Petrie was sheer folly. The man had destroyed many careers in his quest for domination. Tie wouldn't be a match. Shit! I mentally palm-slapped my forehead. I should have sicced Dad on Tie. What had I been thinking asking Maddie to do it? Was there still time?

From the darkening clouds in his eyes, I didn't have to

mention anything about it. Dad was well aware Peter wasn't perfect. That didn't change the fact Peter was his firstborn and heir apparent when Dad retired. Neither Allen nor I showed any inkling to join the family business. If Tie challenged Peter in their marriage, that was one thing. If Tie threatened Peter's reputation—things could get interesting. Quickly.

Had Dad considered Gabe in this equation? From what I knew, Gabe was happy running the Fort Collin's branch of the flower shop and wanted to expand the business. But, if given the chance to join Dad's firm, would he ditch his mother's small-time business compared to Dad's?

"Casey, what should Peter name his child?" Tie smiled sweetly.

I bristled but wasn't sure if it was best to shut down Tie or pray Casey would know how to handle the question.

My father shifted in his seat, looking as if he was weighing the same options.

Casey gave the request some time. "Junior."

Tie forced a laugh. "What if it's a girl?"

"Junior."

"Allen," I jumped in. "I have a conference in Boston during your spring break. Would you like to go?"

"Are you serious?"

I nodded. "It'll be nice to have at least one friendly face in the audience. You will be friendly, right? Historians are a tough crowd."

"I may have some business in New York in the spring. It's possible I could arrange it at the same time and pop down," Dad said. "I love Cambridge. There's a Tex-Mex place in Harvard Square that's kitschy with fantastic margs."

Hearing these tidbits from my father, who for the majority of my life never talked, caught me by surprise even after the past year or so of growing closer. It was like finding out a character in literature had sprung to life and moved into the house next door.

"Sounds great. Just the three of us?" I asked.

"I think so. Peter will have to run things here. And Gabe has made it clear he's not a history guy." Dad almost smiled.

Tie let out a bark of laughter, but no one paid her any attention.

Maddie waltzed in with a notepad. "Who wants what? We have pecan, pumpkin, and apple pie."

"None for me. Need to keep my girlish figure." Tie ran a hand down her side, porn-star style, and it was hard to miss the insinuation that she wasn't pregnant.

"All three, please," Casey said, her hands folded neatly on the table. I wondered if her parents would object to me taking her along for the Harvard trip.

Allen dittoed and proceeded to high-five Casey.

George, who had briefly nodded off, roused enough to request pumpkin before shutting his eyes again. I envied him and hoped he'd stay asleep. Maybe the library tryst with Tie had worn him out in more ways than one.

Orders completed, Maddie slipped out of the room, and try as I might, I couldn't figure out how to guide the conversation without stepping into a Tie landmine.

Uncomfortable silence pressed down on us.

George's body twitched but not enough to wake him.

Allen and I exchanged a look that implied *when will this night end?*

Finally, everyone returned, the women and Gabe laughing. Peter was frowning, but it appeared talking with Ethan had helped some. Or maybe they swapped divorce lawyers' digits.

Maddie announced. "It's official. The roads are closed."

Tie's eyes sought out Peter's, and the sizzle in the air was impossible to ignore.

Sarah placed a hand over her mouth. "Oh, no. I completely forgot to make tea and coffee."

It was understandable, given the night. And did we really want to inject caffeine into anyone present?

The serving crew started to rise again, but I waved for them to take a seat. "Tie, would you help me in the kitchen?"

Sarah stifled a gasp while the rest did their best *did I just hear that right* expressions.

Tie plastered on a sickly-sweet smile and deposited her napkin to the side of her plate. "Would love to."

We made the trek around the table to the door, all eyeballs on us, including Casey's.

I closed the door to the dining room.

"Do I get a cute apron? Like Gabe's but womanlier?" Tie's eyes scouted the kitchen hopefully.

"Knock off the act. I'm going to be very clear." I stepped closer to her, pinning her between the two barstools at the prep station. "Sarah has worked her tail off to plan this evening, cooking all the food, along with Maddie and Rose, so everyone will have a memorable holiday—"

"And, I'm having a great time," she cut me off, situating a hand on my shoulder.

I swiped her hand off. "Cut the crap. Your only mission since arriving in my home has been to sow discord." Unhappy with my word choice, I corrected, "To stir up shit and wreck everyone's night." I waggled my finger in her face. "If you make one more snide comment or false step, I'll personally kick you out of my house. I-25 is closed due to the storm, but there's a hotel within walking distance. If I have to pull you on a sled to get you there, I fucking will."

"You can't kick out your niece's mother on Christmas Eve." She laughed as if that would persuade me the threat was empty.

"Yes, I can. And will."

"You'd kick out Demi?"

"Not Demi. Not Peter. *You*." I poked her shoulder with a finger. "I asked you earlier, for the sake of everyone's holiday, especially for the children's, to table whatever's going on between you and Peter."

"You have no idea what he's done."

"I don't, no. And, I'm not sure it's my business. But I do know I want my children to have a fucking merry Christmas. So, I'll repeat; knock your shit off, or you're out."

"That's not legal. To kidnap my daughter." Her face set to combative level.

I had to give it to her. She knew how to take things to the over-the-top level. "Demi's father is here. And if you think your threat will work, maybe I should inform you that Rose is friends with the chief of police."

She started to speak.

I shook my head. "I don't want to hear it. One more negative thing to come out of your mouth and I'll shove your ass outside. No ifs, ands, or buts." I stretched my fingers past her face to point to the window. "It's really coming down. I sincerely doubt you want to venture far in that. Do you understand me?"

She nodded.

"Good. Fill the teakettle and coffee pot. I'll go take everyone's orders."

CHAPTER ELEVEN

After dessert, the majority of us holed up in the living room to enjoy the fire and Christmas tree.

"Is everyone ready for charades?" Maddie's eyes scouted the living room. "It'll be fun."

I groaned, making my body go limp on the sofa.

Sarah nudged my leg with hers.

Gabe and Allen walked through the front door after seeing George and Gandhi safely home, although both would be back in the morning for gifts and brunch. After his performance at dinner, I nixed the idea of sending anyone to stay at his house. But, Sarah couldn't stand the thought of anyone being alone on Christmas, so the boys would clear a path first thing in the morning if the snow plows hadn't come through.

Noticing the twinkle in Maddie's eye, Gabe asked, "What's up?"

"Charades."

Gabe rubbed his hands together. "Allen and I rock charades, right Bro?"

Allen flashed an evil *we're going to kick everyone's asses* grin.

Helen, Dad, Rose, Troy, and Casey were in the family room

watching *Miracle on 34th Street*, apparently a tradition of my father and Helen's, which was hard to wrap my mind around. When Mom was still alive, did Dad and his secret family celebrate Christmas on a different day to uphold all these traditions? Gabe had mentioned Dad spending Christmas Eve with them, and for the life of me, I couldn't remember if Dad always worked late that night. Or any other nights around Christmas.

"Ethan? Shall we team up?" Maddie asked.

"Oh, thank God, I thought all of you were going to stick me with Lizzie." The evident relief on his face needled me.

"Hey, now. I *am* in the room," I said through gritted teeth.

"Not it," Peter said.

Tie yawned. "I'm too tired."

She looked wide awake to me and conveniently didn't show any signs I'd threatened to kick her out earlier. While I didn't think many would object to my threat, it was still Christmas Eve, and I didn't want to risk permanently being labeled the Grinch.

"I think I'll settle in the library for the night after I take care of some last-minute Christmas morning prep now that we're staying the night." Tie stood as if waiting for someone to plead with her to change her mind.

No one did.

"I set out sheets, pillows, and blankets in the room," Sarah said without looking in Tie's direction.

"Thank you. Peter, can I have the car keys?"

He handed them over, and Tie left with a thin-lipped smile that reminded me so much of the Scotch-lady my insides went stone-cold. I couldn't stop from wondering why she'd ever married Peter. She seemed incapable of love. More like she'd been plotting since the day she first laid eyes on him. How she justified bringing Demi into her conquest was unfathomable to me. Although, I never could figure out why my mother had children either.

When it was safe to speak, Maddie said, "That leaves us with an odd number."

"I'm more than happy to watch." I stretched my arms overhead. "All for the sake of playing fair."

"I'd always known there was something pervy about you," Maddie said, purposefully ignoring my *fair* comment.

"I have an idea." Sarah colored. "Not about Lizzie being a perv. Way too uptight." She squeezed my leg to diminish her words. "We should pit the girls against the boys so everyone can play."

"But we have one extra. Although, Allen is still a babyman." Gabe dodged Allen's shoulder punch.

Maddie sat upright. "Sarah and I are going to clean your clocks."

It didn't escape my notice that I was not factored into the equation, even though it'd been settled I'd be playing. Low expectations were my favorite type.

I suspected Peter wasn't going to play much of a role, either. At times like this, it became quite apparent Peter and I were raised in an unusual household, and the irony of having the last name Petrie, as if we were some scientific experiment, was not lost on me.

"How do we come up with the ideas?" Allen stroked his chin.

"There's a website." Maddie whipped out her phone. "Do you boys want to go first?"

Gage lurched to the center of the room, rubbing his palms together.

"Before we begin, it might help some to know the rules." Maddie elbowed my side. "Each player gives silent clues to their teammates. Should we have a time clock?" she asked Sarah.

Sarah's eyes glanced over me and then Peter. "No. This is for fun. No added pressure."

Or torture.

Peter squirmed in his seat, doing his best to keep his smarmy businessman smile fixed in place. I had to give it to him, considering the day he'd had, and I still hadn't decided how much abuse from Tie he deserved.

Maddie waved Gabe over and showed him the clue.

Gabe palmed the top of his head, nodding in thought. "O-ookay. Not what I was expecting."

"Are you acting, already?" Maddie asked. "Your mind games won't work on us."

It was working on me. Completely.

I wasn't the game playing person at any party, and I wasn't entirely certain I'd ever played charades before. If I had, my mind had blocked out the unpleasant experience. Poker would have been a better choice. I could at least bluff my way through that without the humiliation of pantomime.

Gabe imitated a movie projector.

Allen shouted, "Movie."

Well that was easy, I thought. Maybe I could rock this silly game.

As it turned out, that wasn't the answer, but an indication about what he would be acting out.

I made a mental note of the motion in case my clue was also a movie.

Gabe displayed two fingers.

"Two words." Ethan pressed his palms into his knees, his gangly legs making him look foolish on the petite couch.

Gabe nodded. He held up his index finger.

"One word," Peter said.

Ethan jumped in, "First word."

Ah, that made sense. Maybe this wouldn't be so hard after all. And all I really needed to do was stay one step ahead of Peter. Clearly, our sibling rivalry hadn't tempered even though we were growing closer.

Gabe pointed to his chest.

"You."

"Me."

"Man."

"Boy."

"I," Peter said.

Gabe nodded enthusiastically.

"Fuck," I muttered into my shoulder.

Peter flashed me a cocky big brother grin, which irked and relieved me. I had started to wonder if Tie would break him completely.

"One word, Peter. Still plenty of game," I dished back.

Gabe held two fingers in the air.

"Second word!" Allen was in the charades zone.

Gabe put his hands behind his back and did some type of dance move, although exaggerating he was unsteady.

"Skating," Allen guessed.

Ethan jumped to his feet. *"I, Tonya!"*

Gabe pressed a finger to his nose and then took a victorious bow.

"Lucky guess," Maddie teased.

"Lucky my ass. That was brilliant." Ethan high-fived Gabe and then Peter and Allen.

"All right, girls. Let's show these twerps how it's done." Maddie handed her phone to Gabe. "Give me your best."

"Don't I always?" he replied.

Peter bristled some but remained mute.

Sometimes I forgot just how fucked up my family was on some levels, like Maddie, who'd ditched my brother at the altar, playing charades with her current boyfriend, whom I knew had a diamond ring in his pocket, waiting for the right moment to pop the question.

Dear God, would it happen during the game?

Shoving that thought out of my mind, I turned to Gabe and

Allen, who had lived in the shadows, creating a secret family with my father.

Sarah leaned over and kissed my cheek. "It's okay," she whispered in my ear, and I had to wonder if she was referring to the pressure of the game or if her Sarah Sense had kicked in like it did whenever I drifted away from everyone, plagued by thoughts that were perhaps better left in the past. Maybe the historian in me wouldn't let it. Or my humanness.

Maddie read the clue, her face falling for a brief moment, and I hoped she was simply playing a mind game. Peter would never let me live it down. Although, I still rubbed his nose in the fact that I'd come in third at golf when he'd come in fourth.

She acted out *movie*, which Sarah pounced on. Two words.

Maddie flashed one finger.

"First word," I said with a trace of confidence.

Maddie smiled, holding a forefinger and thumb close together.

Sarah was all over it. "Short. A. It. The."

Maddie gestured it was indeed *The*. Now she stabbed two fingers in the air. She made two fists and tossed punches.

"Punch," I said.

"Fist."

"Swing."

Maddie pointed to her knuckles and made an extension move.

"Super punch," I guessed.

"Knuckle. Claws."

Maddie waved for Sarah to stay with that thought.

Sarah pressed her fingertips into my thigh. *"The Wolverine!"*

Maddie did a happy dance and, not to be outdone by Gabe, did a curtsy fit for meeting Queen Elizabeth the First, not the current occupant of Buckingham Palace.

It was Allen's turn. After receiving his clue, he made a motion that turned out to indicate it was a song.

I noticed Demi fussing on the video monitor. "Be right back." I kissed Sarah's cheek.

"Can't take the pressure, Elizabeth?" Peter mocked.

"Something like that." I climbed the stairs, not bothering to tell him I was checking on his daughter. While Peter adored Demi, I questioned his paternal instincts after dealing with Tie and threatening divorce.

In the nursery, I picked up Demi and snuggled her close to my chest. "Shhh, my little Demitasse." She wiggled in my arms until yawning and settling against me. "You're so delicate, like porcelain, but there's spunk in you like espresso."

Within minutes, she was sound asleep, and I laid her back down, brushing her dark locks off her sleepy-warm forehead.

The game had seemed to elevate to an even more boisterous and competitive level during my absence.

"Ah, Elizabeth. It's your turn." Peter relished this fact more than I thought him capable. Was he feeling somewhat better knowing Tie was down for the night, or had he reached into an inner reserve of prickishness? Or, had my pulling Tie aside relieved him some, knowing he wasn't on his own for what was on the horizon?

I interlaced my fingers and cracked my knuckles, competitor style. "Watch this, Petey."

Maddie and Sarah laughed.

No one called him Petey. Well, maybe Maddie had in the past if I remembered correctly.

"Oh, snap." Gabe held the phone to me, and I read the clue, the two of us huddled with our backs to the group.

I whispered for only him, "Is that a movie?"

Quietly, he informed me it was a song. He added, "You got this." Flipping around, he waved for me to take the floor.

How was it possible that after receiving a PhD, marrying a stunning woman, having twins—all these major life achievements—a simple game of charades rocked me to the core?

Peter attempted to intimidate me by gnashing his teeth.

Allen's eyes darted toward Peter and then me as if saying don't mind him.

Ethan nodded at me, bucking up my nerve.

Maddie wore a dazzling smile.

There was even a brief moment when Peter gave me an encouraging bob of the head, but it was fleeting, or had I imagined it?

And then there was Sarah, sweet, kind, loving, and sexy Sarah, giving me an expression that said *no matter what, I got you.*

I mimed *song*.

Showed two fingers.

Paused.

Which should I start with?

I indicated first word and leaned over, with my hand barely above the carpet.

"Little."

"Short."

"Small."

"Baby."

"Mini."

"Lilliputian," Sarah shouted, and I had to grin.

"You two can be such nerds." She made a gagging sound to indicate our connection made her ill.

I waved for them to keep going.

"Tiny," Sarah said.

I nodded feverishly and let them know I was moving on to the second word. But it entailed something I sucked at and never did unless forced to, like on our wedding day, which nearly resulted in me taking out the cake. And now I had to do it in front of all of them, including Peter.

Then I replayed a memory of dancing naked in front of the fire in our old apartment. My eyes bored into Sarah's. She seemed to connect to me.

I danced.

"'Tiny Dancer!'" she blurted and then hopped to her feet to dash across the room into my arms as if I'd just delivered a knockout blow.

Ethan waved, adding a sarcastic, "Phooey! You two cheated with that couple voodoo shit you have going on."

I had one arm around Sarah. "I think it's time for round two of pie."

Allen hopped up. "Yes!"

"And booze!" Maddie crowed. "It's always time for more eggnog."

The men and Maddie absconded to the kitchen, Peter bringing up the rear, looking back at Sarah and me with an expression I couldn't figure out.

Sarah rested her head on my shoulder. "I'm exhausted."

"Pie and then bed."

"You did well. I know you hate shit like this."

"Which shit are you referring to?"

She laughed. "Good point. This whole day has been a challenge for the likes of you."

"I wouldn't say that. Some cute girl has shown me the error of my lonely ways."

"This cute girl sounds like trouble."

"Most definitely. But so fucking worth it."

"You have it that bad?" Her voice was alluring.

"Want me to take you upstairs and show you just how bad?"

She practically melted in my arms. "Wouldn't that be nice?" She took my right hand in hers. "Come on. Let's get this night over with. At least none of our neighbors took me up on my champagne offer."

I tilted my head back. "I'm pretty sure our entire group had a Shining vibe, and the neighbors feared for their lives coming to our mini-mansion in the likes of this storm."

"I love you, Lizzie, but your family can be trying."

I bumped my hip into hers. "I've been telling you this for years. Are you finally seeing it?"

Her face clouded over. "Do you think Peter has another child on the way?"

I sighed. "I really hope not, but the men in this family seem to play by different rules and expect us…" My voice trailed off.

"Tie doesn't seem to follow rules, either."

"It's hard to know which way is up when it comes to them." I held her in my arms. "I'm so lucky to have you. Please, let's never become anything like them. Vindictive. Cruel. Petty."

"We don't have it in us." She kissed me sweetly on the lips. "Come on. Let's get this party over with."

CHAPTER TWELVE

I woke earlier than usual on Christmas morning after a fitful night of sleep. Dad, Helen, and Allen had stayed with Rose and Troy. But having so many under our roof was more nerve-wracking than living in London during the blitz. Okay, maybe not quite that bad, but I still didn't feel secure.

I attempted to wake Sarah by nuzzling her cheek with my nose. "Merry Christmas, beautiful."

She grumbled and did her best to push me away. "It's early. Turn your light off and go back to sleep."

I ignored her directive. "It is. And it's the only time we'll get to ourselves for the entire day." I kissed her neck, aware it was one of her weaknesses. I had zero shame.

"If you're trying to get laid, think twice about it." She opened one eye. "It's not even six."

"Not trying to get laid, unless it'll improve your mood. Totally willing to take the hit for the team if need be." I continued kissing her neck.

"Sleeping would improve my mood. Why don't you go for a Christmas bike ride or something?"

"Are you giving me the brushoff and seriously suggesting I go for a ride in a blizzard?"

"Are you seriously suggesting you're waking me this early to chat?" Her voice was becoming more playful.

"No, I wanted to give you your gift."

"Again, if you're trying to get laid, grave miscalculation, Mrs. Petrie."

"And I'm telling you, Mrs. Petrie, I'm not. Roll over."

She did so, with more grumbling, although there was a faint smile on her face. "How did I fall in love with a morning person?"

"Either my good looks or charming personality."

"I forgot to mention a *delusional* morning person."

"You're quite sexy, right now." I straddled her waist, with one hand behind my back.

Being completely naked helped my cause, and Sarah took in my flesh with her eyes, her grogginess easing with each passing second. "You're starting to grow on me some. This morning, at least."

I waggled my eyebrows. "Are you ready for your gift?"

She reached between my legs.

I swatted her hand away. "I told you that isn't it."

"It's quite appealing now, though. How do I talk you into it?" She raised her thigh. "Doesn't seem like it'll be all that hard to have my way with you."

I grinned down at her. "Not sure I've ever been able to say no to you, but first, close your eyes."

She refused for several seconds before saying, "Fine."

I dangled the locket over her chest. "You can look now."

Her eyes popped open. "What?" She took it in her hands, tossing me off so she could sit up and inspect it. "Lizzie, this is beautiful."

I curled up next to her. "Open it."

She did. On the right-hand side was a photo of Fred

hugging Ollie, both giggling with such innocent faces. Sarah tapped the left-hand side, which was empty.

"That's for Charlie. Or Charlie one and two if history repeats itself. Turn the locket over."

We'd talked about naming our next child Charlie after my father, since Fred and Olivia's middle names were tributes to her parents.

"Are those initials?" She squinted, flipping on the lamp on her side of the bed to get a better view. "OFC. Does this really read OFC?"

"It does."

"But it's an antique, or I think it is."

"Yes. It was made between the 1880s to 1920s."

"Did you add the engraving?"

I shook my head. "It was meant to be yours after whoever owned it previously, of course."

"Fate."

"Yes, fate."

"Put it on me." She thrust out her neck.

I wrapped the chain around her neck and clasped it. The locket rested right above her chest.

She pressed it close to her heart. "I love it."

"I love you."

"I… didn't get you anything… this sentimental."

"Says the mother of our twins."

She opened the locket again, admiring the photo. "How did I get so lucky?"

"I ask myself that every day, with you in the equation, naturally."

"I think we're both lucky."

I peered over my shoulder. "No one is stirring yet. I think you can squeeze in at least another hour of sleep. I'll head—"

She yanked my face close, smothering my lips with hers.

I pulled away. "Or we can do this."

"What's this?" She fondled my right breast.

"A boob," I deadpanned. "As a lesbian, I'd think you'd be familiar with them. Of course, yours are..." I buried my face in her chest. "We really need to keep sleeping in the nude if this is the end result."

"You really need to shut up and fuck me."

I saluted her, taking her nipple into my mouth.

"I'd recommend speeding things up. It's only a matter of time until someone gets up."

"You're bossy on Christmas mornings. Are you even...?" I stuck my hand between her legs, feeling her wetness. "That's a yes, then. Who knew lockets had this effect on you?" I shoved two fingers inside while I kissed her.

Our breathing rapidly increased.

Being inside her—so fucking good. I let out a moan.

"Shhh. Don't wake anyone until..."

There was a sound, but it turned out to be a gust of wind battering the north side of the house.

I quickened the pace of my fingers, trailing my tongue down her stomach. She'd need both penetration and oral to get there in a hurry, and her urgent writhing telegraphed she desired a quick release.

My tongue landed on her clit.

Sarah gyrated her hips, doing all she could to help the process. Or maybe to complain I hadn't accomplished her goal quite yet. She could be impatient sometimes. But could she really blame me for wanting to take my time pleasuring her?

"That feels good," she whispered when I drove in deep. "Keep that up."

I did, matching my hammering efforts with my tongue.

"Ohhh..."

I went in deep, keeping my fingers there, circling her clit with my tongue in the way I knew would tip her over the edge.

Her legs quaked.

Her back arched.

She released a tiny moan that I wished could have been full throttle, but given the house full of guests, it wasn't possible.

I pressed my tongue against her clit to extend the sensation, and her body jerked.

Several moments later, her body stilled.

Our bedroom door rattled.

Sarah yanked the covers over us, and I flattened as much as possible.

The door squeaked open, reminding me I needed to WD-40 the hinges.

Casey's voice squealed, "It's Christmas!"

"It is, sweetheart. Go wake your daddy, and we'll get going." Sarah sounded remarkably calm, considering.

"Where's Lizzie?" Her voice sounded closer.

"In the bathroom. We'll meet you in the kitchen. Can you close the door on your way out? Thanks."

"Hurry up!" The door clicked into the jamb, and her footsteps retreated down the hallway.

Sarah lifted the covers, her face aflame. "Maybe we should start locking our door."

"Or not have people stay over all the time."

"There's that, but with our friends and family, a lock sounds like the simplest solution." She moaned. "I had intended to…" She made a motion, which I assumed was meant to say reciprocate.

"Yeah, sure. I've heard that one before. Is it safe to come out? It's kind of hard to breathe."

"Oh, sorry." She yanked the covers off. "We better get downstairs before this day gets away from us like yesterday." Sarah slid into her robe and headed to the bathroom.

Sitting on the edge of the bed while Sarah hopped in the shower, I strained to hear if any other creatures, besides Casey, were stirring, and if there were, I was praying for Christmas mice. Was that how the poem went?

For the umpteenth time, I was reminded of my childhood deficit, as Maddie liked to say. While millions of American children had parents who read them nighttime stories, I had the Scotch-lady, who ignored my existence to the best of her alcohol-soaked abilities. And, Dad had been too busy raising Gabe and Allen. I wondered how committed Sarah was to naming our next child Charlie.

Assured no one else was up, I tossed on jeans and a long sleeve and decamped downstairs after a quick trip to the bathroom on the main floor.

Casey sat in a chair at the kitchen table, munching on Cheerios she'd poured into a bowl without milk or a spoon. She popped one into her mouth with her fingers.

"Morning," I whispered, adding, "Merry Christmas," as I filled the kettle with water from the kitchen sink.

"Do you think Santa came to my house?" She lobbed another Cheerio into her mouth, kicking her feet under the table.

I clicked on the gas burner under the teakettle, stalling for time. How did brainiac Casey still believe in Santa? "Are you worried you won't have any gifts to open when you get home?"

"Daddy said Santa was dead-broke due to the Republican tax bill." She munched on another Cheerio, not showing much disappointment. "Do elves get health benefits? Is being short a preexisting condition?"

I placed my hand over the spout of the kettle as if using my mental powers to heat up the water faster. This wasn't the type of conversation I wanted to have, especially before getting my first dose of caffeine. "Oh, I think Santa treats his elves quite well."

"Hmm." She pointed out the window. "I haven't seen any reindeer tracks."

I pivoted slowly. "Have you been up all night?"

Casey nodded. "Last year, I fell asleep, but not this one."

"And you never saw reindeer or Santa?" It was fruitless to stall yet again, but I was out of my depth.

"Oh, I heard something around one o'clock in the front of the house, but I wasn't sure if I should inspect. Daddy said if Santa spied me peeking, all my presents would disintegrate. Is that possible?" Without waiting for a reply, she continued, "That's why I was in here, keeping an eye out for reindeer. Can they fly during a blizzard?"

At least she hadn't spied Sarah and me setting out gifts under the tree, crushing her belief in Santa. It was difficult to wrap my head around all the fibs Ethan had to concoct daily to deal with his overly inquisitive daughter. The kettle started to whistle, but I whisked it off the flame before alerting the rest of the house Christmas morning had started. "Most definitely. They're reindeer, after all, and thrive in these conditions." I jerked my head to the window at the piles of snow outside that I couldn't see since it was still black as midnight and all the Christmas lights had been switched off long ago.

Her expression didn't elicit much confidence in my assertion. She hopped off the kitchen chair and wandered to my side, still clutching the Cheerios bowl. Not wanting to talk down to her while I fixed my breakfast, I hoisted her onto the island.

"Would you like some fruit and toast?" I pulled out the drawer next to the oven, which was the toaster's home.

"I like bananas."

"Righty-O." I picked a ripening banana from the fruit bowl. "Is this yellow enough?"

She nodded. "Did you know giraffes eat dirt?"

While cracking the banana open for her, I pondered the meaning of her question. Was she literally talking about giraffes, or was this a comment she heard from the likes of

Maddie referring to... what? Lesbian sex? "Would you like me to chop up banana on top of your cereal?"

Casey shook her head. "I don't like my food touching other food."

"Does that include milk?"

"Correct."

I wondered if this trait would outlast her childhood.

"So, did you know that about giraffes?" She set the bowl down on the counter and accepted the peeled banana.

I slotted two pieces of seeded bread into the toaster. "Nope. Where did you hear that?"

"From Ian. He's in my dance class, and he has a faux mohawk." She mimed spiking up her hair on top. "Should I cut my hair short so I can do that?"

Not wanting to step into the hair-style landmine, I asked, "How does Ian know so much about giraffes?" I bit into a crunchy Gala apple.

"His mom, not his birth mom but lesbian mom, is a world traveler."

Again, that roused my suspicions that the giraffe licking dirt comment was a lesbian thing, but how could I ask Casey for clarification?

I opted to tiptoe around the issue. "Why do they eat dirt?"

"For minerals."

Somewhat mollified, I nodded. "Like taking vitamins."

"Exactly. I'm glad I don't have to eat dirt for my iron and zinc intake."

Luckily the toast sprang up, allowing me to turn my back to hide my smile. Never in a million years did I think I'd be spending Christmas morning chatting with a child about giraffes eating dirt for minerals. Wait. Why was no one up yet?

I smeared vegan butter onto a slice of toast. "It's awfully quiet, don't you think?"

"Daddy warned me he'd be late today. He says it's Maddie's fault."

"What's my fault?" Maddie strolled into the kitchen, yawning, with little Demi on her hip.

"Everything, according to Ethan," I said. "But in this case, I think your eggnog."

Sarah trailed in after Maddie with a twin on each hip. "Coffee and stat." She added, "Please."

"Merry Christmas," I said with too much vindictive glee. "Did you know giraffes eat dirt? Casey, fill them in while I get going on the twins' breakfast and coffee for the grown-ups."

Casey hopped down from the island.

While prepping the coffee, Sarah sidled up next to me for a cuddle after securing the twins and Demi in their high chairs.

I took advantage of the opportunity and whispered in her ear, "Casey's worried Santa didn't know where to find her. She stayed up all night. And we, rather Dad dressed as Santa, gave her our gift last night."

"We can commandeer gifts from others that are suitable." Turning around, she addressed Maddie. "Would you help Lizzie feed the kids while I treat myself to a soak in the tub before all the Christmas madness starts."

Maddie asked, "Didn't you just—?"

Sarah placed a finger to her lips.

"Got it. Help Lizzie and mind my own business."

Sarah's back was to me, but her eye roll was easy to detect without the benefit of sight.

Maddie laughed.

* * *

I MADE a quick sweep of the main floor to see if anyone else was up. Ethan stood in front of the unlit Christmas tree, looking as if he hadn't slept in days.

"Out of curiosity, did Casey ask Santa for any particular gifts?" I asked in a hushed tone.

Ethan's eyes fell to the floor. "A laptop."

"And...?"

His eyes met mine. "What do you think?"

"I think Santa heard her request."

He started to protest.

I waved that it was useless. "I'm going to take advantage of your hangover and play the *her mother isn't here* card. Besides, that happens to be one of the gifts we can accommodate at the drop of a hat."

"You just happen to have a brand-new laptop laying around?"

"In a way. It's for Allen, but he adores Casey so I doubt he'll argue. I'm putting coffee on. You in?" I breezed by him on the way back to the kitchen. "Would you mind plugging in the tree? It's Christmas morning, after all. Fa la la and all that hoopla."

He complied and then followed me. "You seem chipper for this early. I hate you."

"Aw, Merry Christmas to you too, buddy." I winked at him.

Maddie must have moved the kiddos and Casey to the dining room, where there was more space for the feeding frenzy.

"Do you think we can make it to your house to pack some clothes or—?"

He raised a hand and gave me the once-over. "You had sex, didn't you? I doubly hate you."

I balked. "You hate sex."

"I hate couples who like each other these days, and having sex implies liking. Dare I even say love?"

He had me there, but to help ease his worried mind, I decided to play the game. I darted my eyes upward. "It's not even seven in the morning. Do you really think we got up super early to get our groove on? After the shitstorm of yesterday?"

"You two, most definitely. The sickly-sweet couple with the perfect family." He rocked on his heels, his arms crossed.

"If you think the Petries are perfect, I really don't want to meet your parents."

"You know what I mean."

"Come now. Lisa's going to be thrilled to see you tonight. We should head out soon after opening the presents. Who knows what the roads will be like?"

"It's going to take a lot more than showing up." He sighed and vamoosed.

Unfortunately, he was correct, but baby steps had helped me in the past when I needed to get my life back together.

Gabe walked in, his hands pressed together. "What can I help with?"

"Have a man-to-man chat with Ethan."

He started to laugh but curbed it when he gathered I was serious. "Got it. I'll go find him."

"My guess is the family room since Peter and Tie are in the library. And I suggest waiting for the coffee."

The two of us worked on getting caffeine flowing for all the adults. Part of me wouldn't be surprised if Casey requested an espresso. The thought of her brain firing even more synapses worried me, though.

Sarah, in jeans and a cable-knit sweater, yawned. "Morning, Gabe. How'd you sleep?"

"Better than Ethan. She"—he jerked his thumb at me—"is making me have a *mano-a-mano* chat with him." He grabbed two of the cups. "Wish me luck."

"Do I want to know?" Sarah scooped two spoons of sugar into her drink. This didn't send me into a panic like it had yesterday because she treated herself to sugar on special days.

"I'm thinking Ethan may snap before I take him to the airport."

She wrapped her arms around my waist. "That was sweet of you. To buy his ticket."

"He'd do the same for me if he could."

"True, but it does surprise me sometimes when you don't need me to tell you what to do."

I laughed. "This is my thanks for this morning."

"Another round may get me to be a smidge nicer."

"I'll see what I can work out. Maybe send the family out for a walk, and fingers crossed they'll reenact the Donner Party."

She laughed.

"I mentioned your idea of commandeering gifts for Casey. Ethan approved of Allen's laptop."

"What about the printer?"

"I spaced the printer, but they kinda go together so…" I shrugged, adding, "Besides, Casey really should have both. Everyone else was expected to return on Christmas morning, so we have gifts for them. Casey still believes in Santa. Let her keep a hold of her innocence for a little longer. God knows things may get rough in her house."

Sarah mulled this over, finally nodding her assent.

"How much more coffee do we need?" I asked.

"Mom, Troy, and their party are on their way on foot. They can't get their car out of the snowbank Troy wedged it into last night. George will be over once the men dig a path." She opened the pantry and pulled out a cardboard box. "This will help."

I read the label. "Plastic two pot airpot station. You've got to be kidding me. This isn't a bank lobby. It's our home."

"Don't start. There will be thirteen adults. I don't want to spend the entire morning fetching coffee for everyone."

"I don't drink coffee."

"But you know where the tea stuff is." She kissed my cheek.

"I'm going to help Maddie get the twins in their outfits. Can I trust you with this?" She patted the top of the box but didn't wait for a response before leaving.

I opened the box and read the directions.

The doorbell rang, but I allowed someone else to get it.

Moments later, Peter's booming voice in the living room caused a cold sensation. Were he and Tie already at each other's throat before the first gift was unwrapped?

I finished setting up the coffee station on the hutch in the dining room.

"Lizzie!" Tie's morning greeting was overly exuberant, coupled with her tossing her arms around me, giving each of my cheeks a sloppy kiss.

Was she drunk?

"Coffee?" I made a ta-da motion to the setup.

"Would love some. Black, please." She moved on to say hello to Maddie and the kids, including her own daughter, whom we were taking care of.

"So much for the self-service station," I muttered.

"Complaining?" Sarah sidled up to me.

"I think Tie's drunk or acting weirder than normal. Also, she refused to make her own cup of coffee. Black coffee I might add. All she had to do was pour." I reached for one of the containers and did exactly that.

Sarah clasped her fingers around the locket. "Just keep replaying this morning in your head to get through the day."

I laughed. "You want me to think about sex with you while around the Petries?"

"It's how I've survived many fraught dinners." She gave me a peck on the cheek and whirled around to greet her mom and Troy.

Dad and Helen, blurry eyed and pale, approached, still in yesterday's clothes but freshly showered.

"I need to get something like this for the flower shops."

Helen eyed the coffee station from all angles. "Were did you find it?"

"I'm assuming the behemoth we get packages from nearly every day."

"So do we," Dad grumbled. Clearly the holiday spirit hadn't bitten him yet.

"Not all of us have a driver we can send out to get things." Helen poured a cup, taking the creamer and sugar packets to the living room.

"Trouble?" I asked.

He shrugged. "I... Does anyone deliver on Christmas? My gift didn't go over well."

I sidled closer. "What'd you get her?"

"Cooking classes," he grumbled.

I sucked in my lips. "Did she want them?"

"Years ago, she mentioned it, but I don't think she remembers, or quite possibly, she thinks the gift implied I wish she was more of a homemaker. So delivery...?" He shoved his hands into his pockets, rattling some coins.

I did what Sarah suggested and thought of climbing on top of my wife's body, feeling my skin on hers. The warmth. Love. Bliss. "I don't know, but most stores probably deliver tomorrow. It's never too late to make Helen happy."

He grunted, pouring a cup. "Is it possible to make a woman happy?"

"From my experience, yes." I smiled over the memory of giving Sarah her gift earlier.

Dad followed my eyes to Sarah. "She's a lovely woman."

"That she is. Yesterday, Peter told me she brings out the best in me."

"I agree with that assessment."

"I think Helen has for you." I crossed my arms and rocked on my feet. "It's difficult knowing you... got a second chance for a family with her, Allen, and Gabe, while Peter and I—well, you know it wasn't easy in our house. With Mom. She hated me and used Peter. While I wish that had been different, I have to wonder what I would have done in your shoes had I'd met Sarah after getting married. Hopefully the right thing, but given all the moving parts—vindictive wife, two children, running a company—who can say for sure what the right thing is, really? Humans. We complicate the shit out of everything." I sucked in a breath. "I guess what I'm trying to say is I think Helen was always the right fit for you and I'm happy you found her."

He stared at me, his mouth agape. "I should have done more. For you and Peter."

"It's never too late. I'm right here. And Peter, he really needs a father right now."

He stared at me before wrapping his arms around me for a tight but brief squeeze. "Thank you, Lizzie. I'm continually amazed by how you turned out to be such a strong and loving woman. Even to those who hurt you. Including me." He took a breath. "Would you excuse me?" He approached Peter across the room and gave him a hug.

"My job here is done," I said with a faint smile.

While in the kitchen, Gandhi rushed up to me, jumping on my legs. I scooped him up into my arms and was rewarded with wet kisses. "At least someone is genuinely happy to see me this morning."

He squirmed, so I set him down, and he dashed off for his next victim.

Casey tugged on my hand. "Is it time yet?"

"Let's go see if everyone is here."

She held onto my hand.

In the living room, I spied three groups of people. Allen, Dad, Helen, and Peter, who was holding Demi, huddled near the door to the veranda. George, Tie, and Maddie were stationed next to the fire, which was already going. Sarah and Troy, each with a twin on one of their hips, stood with Rose.

No Ethan or Gabe, who had cleared a path for George but clearly had decamped to the library now that Peter and Tie were on the loose.

I made eye contact with Sarah, who handed off Fred to Maddie and said, "Casey, can you help me get the gifts ready this morning?"

Casey dashed over to Sarah, and I headed for the library—command central when shit hit the fan.

Before entering, I peeked in to gauge the situation.

The men sat on opposing couches, not speaking, remnants of sheets and blankets shoved on the carpet.

So much for *mano-a-mano*.

I knocked on the open door, my head poking around. "Everyone is here. Are you two ready for gifts?"

Gabe stood and stretched his hands over his head, tugging his T-shirt above his pajama bottoms, showing his abs. I was certain he'd changed back into his pajamas after shoveling, more than likely since his jeans were wetter than wet given the amount of snow. "Try to stop me."

Maddie and Gabe were the only ones who'd packed emergency bags in case the weather turned nasty. Not to mention Maddie had plenty of clothes and toiletries here for when she stayed over.

On his way out, he whispered, "It's bad. He and Lisa talked on the phone last night after we all went to bed, and well…" He hitched a shoulder.

That explained the major difference in his mood since purchasing the airline ticket.

I entered the room, not knowing what I should say or do.

Ethan wiped his eyes. "Almost ready," he said.

"I understand." I took a seat.

"How's Casey?" he asked.

"Helping Sarah organize or something."

He smiled. "Right up Casey's alley."

"Same with Sarah."

"I'm sorry about earlier. It's just…"

"Already forgotten, Ethan. You never have to apologize to me. Isn't that the definition of friendship? Maddie has that on a coffee mug, which I think makes her believe she's covered for all of her jabs at me."

He laughed. "You are her favorite target."

"I've noticed that."

"She means well."

"At least seventy percent of the time."

He laughed harder.

I stood. "Come on. Let's help our children have their Christmas. There's time later for…" I left the rest unsaid.

"I don't want to bother going to my house to pack. I just want to get there." He rose and wrapped me into his arms. "Thank you, Lizzie."

CHAPTER THIRTEEN

Freddie sat in Sarah's lap on the floor by the tree. Ollie was with Maddie.

Casey rooted behind the tree on her hands and knees. "Who's first?"

"Freddie and Ollie," Sarah said.

Casey pulled out one wrapped gift and placed it before Ollie. She spied her dad and said, "I'm playing Santa!"

"And doing an excellent job." He placed a tender kiss on the top of her head before skirting around the Dickens village.

Maddie waved him over to sit next to her and Ollie on the floor. His knees jutted in weird contortions as he settled on the beige carpet.

Casey plunked a gift down for Freddie.

Ollie had already torn through the wrapping paper, more enthused by shredding the paper into tiny pieces than the present itself.

Fred appraised his gift, his eyes wide. He seemed to be calculating the best method to tackle the task at hand. Or perhaps, he didn't want to spoil it.

Casey's large eyes implored Sarah. "Next?"

"Casey and Demi."

"He found me!" She zipped back behind the tree.

"I could use ten of her in my shop," Helen joked.

"She helps me with everything, including balancing the checkbook," Ethan added.

No one questioned the veracity of his claim.

Soon enough, the entire room was covered with discarded ribbons, bows, and wrapping paper. I tried to keep up with the mess, making a swing through with a trash bag to pick up the scraps, but Freddie and Ollie rolled around in the destruction on the floor, giggling. Demi sat in a bouncy chair, smiling, and Gandhi licked all their faces.

Hank wandered into the room, looked around, and sauntered out with his tail turned up.

Maddie had her phone out, recording the kids. Casey had placed a bow on the little ones' heads, declaring, "You're gifts now."

Sarah and I stared into each other's eyes, completely agreeing with Casey's words.

"The best gifts," Peter said, much to my surprise.

Dad reached for Helen's hand, who gave it a tight squeeze.

Rose leaned into Troy's chest.

Tie and Peter sat as far away from each other as possible.

Ethan's phone lit up, and soon enough Lisa was on Facetime, wishing everyone a Merry Christmas.

"Mommy!" Casey zipped over and grabbed the phone. "I got a laptop, printer, and a copy of *Little Women*." She disappeared into the library, Ethan following.

When I had explained the situation to Allen, he didn't mind one bit about giving Casey the laptop and printer. The special edition of *Little Women* was the one Sarah had given me when we moved into our house.

Sarah stood. "I'll get going with brunch."

"I'll help you." Maddie rose along with Helen.

Gabe opened Ollie's Thomas and Friends Railway Pals Destination Discovery. "Shall we put this together, Ollie?"

She nodded. Freddie stacked his new blocks, with pictures of an owl, badger, hedgehog, deer, fox, and rabbit.

Demi had wrapping paper sticking out of her mouth, which I removed.

"Allen, can you grab another trash bag from the kitchen?" I asked.

He set aside the hardcover book about the Russian Revolution I'd given him after having the visiting Harvard professor autograph it to Allen. I think it was the first time the eminent historian was asked to sign his book.

Peter took an imaginary practice swing with the new golf glove Sarah and I got him.

Casey and Ethan returned from the library.

"Casey, help Lizzie gather all the paper," Ethan said.

"Allen will help you when he gets back with another garbage bag. Ethan, we should think about leaving in a couple of hours or so."

"Gotcha. Anyone need coffee?" Only receiving shakes of the head, Ethan strode to the coffee command center in the dining room.

Helen waltzed in and said something to my father.

Casey spied my system, sorting bows and ribbons that weren't too badly damaged, and got to work. Some of the carnage ended up under the tree, and once again she was on her hands and knees. "Oh, there's one last gift. It's for you, Uncle Peter."

Tie's face lit up.

That didn't compute in my brain until Peter tore through the paper, his face going ashen, then quickly turning scarlet, resulting with the veins in his forehead bulging. His mouth opened and closed, working up to an epic meltdown.

Helen, with her usual keen eye, removed the frame from his

hands, handed it to me without looking at it, and ushered Peter out of the room to avoid a scene in front of the children.

Ethan sidled up as I held the frame to see what the hubbub was about. I hadn't expected to get an eyeful of Peter in bed with a woman who was most certainly not Tie. Ethan and I exchanged *what the fuck* looks.

Tie sat in the wingback chair, her legs crossed, hands on knees as if sitting for a family portrait.

I wasn't the violent type, but I had an urge to smash her and Peter in the face. Not wanting to give either the satisfaction, I tossed the questionable gift into the trash bag and continued the cleanup process without saying a word.

Sarah, as if in tune with the turmoil, called me into the kitchen.

Dad nodded, indicating he'd watch the little ones.

Gabe had all three's rapt attention, guiding their little fingers in attaching the forty-piece set. I gave Ollie another three minutes before she abandoned the project, but Fred would stay to the bitter end.

"Can you help me get the serving dishes?" Sarah asked.

I reached into the trash bag and pulled out Tie's surprise.

Maddie craned over Sarah's shoulder, gasping. "It's the same one."

"The same what?" I asked without thinking.

"I have a photo similar to that one."

Sarah and I gawked at Maddie. "You hired a private investigator?" she asked.

"I had to know the truth before the wedding." Maddie took the frame from me, inspecting it.

It made sense, why she'd waited until the big day, ditching him at the altar. I had no idea how I would react if I had a photo of Sarah with another woman. Lose my fucking mind. But wrap it and present it as a Christmas gift in front of the entire family—that was going too fucking far. Peter clearly didn't make wise decisions, refused to learn from his mistakes, and the women in his life had his number when it came to humiliating him. He deserved a reckoning. Of that I had no doubt. But in front of Demi. My twins. And all our guests. That was too much for me.

Not wanting to lose sight of the real matter at hand, I said, "Helen's with Peter in the library."

"On it." Maddie left, with her hand still clutching the frame.

"Is she going to Peter, Tie, or… is there a third option?" I asked.

Sarah raised one shoulder. "She has a habit of inserting herself into Peter's life. Or do you not recall when she and Peter stayed the night here?"

I did remember them sleeping together in my home. Something like that was difficult to erase from my delicate memory bank.

I stabbed a useless finger in the air and looked helplessly to Sarah. "I had hoped you or someone else who hasn't slept with Peter would go, instead of the other jilted woman." I paused. "No, Peter was cast away. What would the word be for Maddie? And is she going to the library to be helpful or for round two or whatnot concerning this mystery woman." How many words could I think of for a vindictive woman? Vengeful, mean, petty, hurtful, spiteful… I pulled out my phone and googled more synonyms. One site listed over three hundred.

Sarah sighed and placed a hand on each of my shoulders. "Don't disappear on me, Lizzie. Not with this going on."

"What?" I asked.

I'd been lost in thought, and Dad surprised me when he spoke. "What's going on?"

I hid my phone behind my back for some inexplicable reason, as if that would bust what was happening with Peter, not just my nerdy vocab side. "Uh, we're working on brunch. Should be ready soon. You hungry? I'm famished myself."

"What's going on with Tie and Peter?"

"N-nothing," I stuttered.

"What are you hiding behind your back?"

"N-nothing."

He showed his palm for me to place my phone in his hand, not speaking but commanding with his eyes.

I shook my head.

Sarah was frozen.

He didn't relent, saying my full name in what I imagined was his dad-like voice, taking into account it was the first time I recalled hearing it.

I gave in and handed it over, relieved I wasn't holding the picture.

He scrunched his brow. "Tie? Are you looking up words for her?"

"Possibly Maddie," I conceded with a shrug.

He nodded, understanding more than I thought he would. Although, he'd have to be a total nincompoop not to pick up on Tie's jabs for the past fourteen hours or so. And surely he knew why Maddie had called off the wedding. Her note about giving the dress to the other woman hadn't been meant to be subtle.

Dad headed off toward the library.

"What do we do?" I asked.

"I want them out of my house," Sarah said through gritted teeth. "I've had it with the Petries."

I looked through the kitchen window. "There's a foot of snow on the roads, and it's Christmas."

"I don't care what day it is." She crossed her arms.

"Not that. I don't think the plows are in full force. How do I get them out of here?"

"Open the door and point your finger."

I stepped back. "Me?"

"You were in their wedding."

"So that means I have to toss them out? You're the one who always insists on having family time."

"This is my responsibility?" She placed a hand over her heart.

"I-I don't want to do it," I stuttered yet again. "They scare me."

"Well, she scares the shit out of me! Peter—he's been difficult to read lately."

We stood in the kitchen, daring the other to act.

Finally, she said, "This is ridiculous."

"Are you going to do it then?"

"No. They should leave on their own accord to deal with their problems."

"If this were a normal marital spat between two normal people, I would agree. But this is Peter and Tie. I don't think they should ever be in the same room together again."

Tie came into the kitchen. "How can I help with brunch?"

I started to make a fist, but Sarah clasped her hand over mine. "We're almost done. Can I get you anything?"

I gave Sarah a *what the fuck* look.

She dished it back.

Tie took in Sarah's face and then mine. "I don't want to trouble you two with everything going on. I'll get myself a refill on coffee."

When alone, I asked, "What was that about? *Can I get you something?*" I mimicked Sarah's voice.

"I panicked, okay?"

Ethan casually strolled in as if trying not to be noticed but dying to know what was going on. He stirred the bacon in the frying pan.

Sarah joined him at the stove, shoveling hash browns onto one of the platters. "Lizzie, can you get the muffins and croissants out?"

"Sure. I can do that." I glanced around the kitchen. "Where are they?"

Sarah groaned, throwing the spatula onto the hash browns. "Do I have to do everything?"

She stormed around the island to the pantry, pulling out two plastic containers of croissants and an assortment of individual-size coffee cakes and muffins.

I took them from her hand. "Ethan and I got this. Why don't you go into the living room? Check on the kiddos? Have a mimosa?" Or five.

"Do we have those?" Her eyes were hopeful.

Ethan opened the fridge. "One coming right up just for you."

I shoved Sarah out of the kitchen.

Ethan asked, "Do you have Grand Marnier?"

"Uh," I looked at Sarah's retreating back.

"Jesus, Lizzie. Woman up." Ethan shook his head and then extended a long finger. "Go into the library and look."

I was starting to hate the library but knew he was right. I had to step up my game for everyone's sake. Odd, coming from Ethan, who was flying later to be there for his wife.

I quietly knocked on the library door and entered with cold dread expanding in my gut. Dad and Helen sat on one couch and Peter on the other, no one speaking. No sign of Maddie, making me wonder where she'd rushed off to. Had Peter tossed her out? Helen? Dad? Had she lost her nerve? Or remembered she was with Gabe at the moment?

"Sorry," I said. "Just need to check something." At the bar, I scanned the bottles until I found the one I sought. "Thanks."

I returned to the kitchen, holding the bottle victoriously in the air.

Ethan finished the drink, kissing his fingertips with a flourish. "Get this to your wife, stat." He appeared lost in thought. "I'm assuming brunch will have to wait." He shrugged because who the hell knew what was going to happen next? "I'll put everything in the oven to stay warm, and then we'll get the kids dressed to go outside. It's snowman or snowwoman time. I think I'd like to do that with Casey and all of you before leaving for the airport." He got to work.

I gave his shoulder a squeeze on my way out of the kitchen.

In the living room, Sarah had Ollie on her lap, soothing our daughter.

"Here you go, my dear, and you, young lady, come with me." I handed off the drink and scooped up Ollie before Sarah could say anything. The way she sucked down her drink didn't allow her the chance to speak.

A minute or so later, Ethan appeared and swooped up Fred and Demi. "Casey, help us get the twins and Demi ready to play in the snow."

Sarah mouthed *thank you* to both of us.

"What do you think, Ollie Dollie? Can you help Mommy build a snow person?"

Olivia, face still red from a fit, cocked her head, intrigued. I couldn't help it; I squeezed her tightly in my arms, thankful my entire world wasn't falling apart like Peter's in the library.

In the nursery, I pulled out a penguin snowsuit for each twin, handing one to Ethan. "Thank you for stepping in."

Digging in the back of the closet, I found an older snowsuit that would fit Demi. Mostly.

"It's what family is for." He flipped around, his voice cracking.

"Okay, Ollie. Let's get you suited and booted."

"What do you think is being decided?" Ethan asked as he wrestled the wiggly Fred.

"Goodness knows with Peter, Tie, Helen, and my dad involved. So many conflicting relationship dynamics it's hard for me to fully understand. I'm slightly terrified to find out."

Casey came in, dressed for the artic. "Let's get this show on the road!"

"The snow show," Ethan said with a mischievous grin.

Casey laughed, clapping and acting very much like the child she was, not the brainiac.

Ethan, with Fred and Demi on his hips, said, "Come on, kiddos. Nothing's going to stop this Christmas from being jolly."

Out in the backyard, we traversed the shoveled path, which Allen had tackled earlier so Gandhi wouldn't have trouble going to the bathroom outside instead of in my house.

I nearly broke out into hysterical laughter. How had I, the self-proclaimed orphan, ended up with family—a totally crazy family at that—coming out my ying-yang on Christmas morning.

Ethan sucked a deep breath of the frigid air into his lungs. "So pure. And the wind has finally stopped."

"Maybe the storm has passed."

We both peeked through the breakfast nook window, knowing that wasn't true inside.

A snowball crashed into Ethan's back, and he flipped around to see Casey disappear behind a tree. Setting both kids down, Ethan squatted on his haunches, and he and Freddie gathered snow. Well, Freddie poked his gloved fingers at the snow, letting Ethan do all the work. And Demi sat with her chubby legs straight out, grinning.

"What do you say, baby girl? Can you make a snow angel for Mommy?" I placed Ollie on the snow and motioned for her to move her arms and legs.

Freddie, with one eye squinted, took in Ollie's move, showing zero interest in joining in. He was definitely the observer of the two, and I wondered what they'd be like as teenagers. The thought, though, was like a dagger to the gut.

No need to rush the process. The days were already zipping by. I wanted to make the most out of each one.

A snowball rammed into me, splattering flakes onto a giggling Olivia.

I wheeled about to spy Maddie waggling guilty fingers in her typical proud southern way.

"I should have known." I packed my hands with what I hoped was a decent-size retort, not having much experience with snowball warfare. "You brought this upon yourself, Maddie."

She ducked behind Ethan.

Sarah stepped out in her Norwegian ski sweater and snow pants. Winking at me, she made quick work of forming a snowball in her hands and pelting Maddie in the back.

Laughing, Maddie declared, "This means war."

"Don't forget us." Gabe grinned.

Allen had a plotting expression.

I was frozen.

Until Maddie creamed me again.

Then Casey got me.

"No quarter, you two," I said in my most intimidating voice.

Sarah laughed. "For the non-historians, that means she's not taking any prisoners."

"Tough talk for a rookie." Maddie dove behind a snow mound.

Not wanting to get distracted, I positioned Olivia and Demi next to the deck railing to protect them. Sitting on her bum, Ollie applauded, clapping with her hands over her head every time anything white flew by. Demi continued to grin.

Ten feet away, Freddie giggled.

Again, I wondered how I'd ended up here. How did I ensure it would never end?

A blast of snow from above covered the two of us. Brushing

it away from my eyes, the stunning vision of my laughing wife became clear. I stood on my tippy-toes and kissed her.

"Ew," Casey squealed.

Ethan got us both right in the kisser.

"Nicely done," Maddie crowed before hitting him in the face.

Gabe tossed Maddie over his shoulder, taking her to the largest pile of snow in the corner of the yard, looking as if he had every intention of tossing her right into the middle of it.

Maddie shouted, "Don't you dare."

"Or what?" he demanded.

"I'll kill you." She tried freeing herself.

"I'd rather you marry me."

Maddie, still draped over his shoulder, stopped squirming. "What?"

Everyone outside, including the children, went quiet.

"Marry me?" Gabe repeated in a firmer voice.

"Put me down," Maddie said in a strangely calm voice.

He shook his head. "Not until you answer."

"Gabe. Put me down right this minute."

He did.

Sarah slipped her hand into mine.

"Ask me again." Maddie still exhibited the definition of calm.

Gabe smiled, getting on one knee. Biting the end of his glove, he yanked it off and reached into his jean pocket. Holding the ring out to her, he simply said, "I adore you. Marry me?"

It was the simplest of questions that would alter both of their lives.

Sarah squeezed my hand vice-like, cutting off the blood supply.

Ethan and Allen arched their brows at each other.

Maddie still hadn't spoken. Was she thinking of Peter?

Questioning how well she knew Gabe? Or wondering if she really wanted to settle down with someone after everything that'd happened over the past twenty-four hours? The Petries had a way of breaking people.

Gabe never stopped grinning, returning to his usual cocky persona.

Finally, Maddie said, "I'd been considering asking you."

"You still can. I'm an equal opportunity type of guy." He raised two hands in the air, giving her the opportunity.

"I don't have a ring for you."

"I don't need one. All I need is you, Maddie. Forever."

"But you think I do?" In typical female fashion, she ignored the heartfelt part of his declaration.

This had to be one of the weirdest proposals I would ever witness firsthand.

"I do," he said with the confidence of a man in love.

Maddie sucked her bottom lip into her mouth. "Well, are you going to put it on my finger, then?"

Sarah's grip was deathlike now, and she kissed my cheek, tears starting to stream down her face.

Ethan clamped a hand on Allen's shoulder.

Rose stuck her head out the door. "What's going on?"

Sarah turned and said, "Maddie said yes."

Rose edged outside. "It's about time. Gabe has been tying himself into knots for the past two days."

Troy stepped out beside her and raised her hand to his lips, and there was a ring on Rose's hand. How had I not noticed before? Or anyone? The Petrie effect?

I peeked at Sarah to get a temperature on if she'd spied the rock.

Sarah rested her head on my shoulder and whispered, "You weren't the only one who woke a woman early to give a Christmas gift."

"Ah, that's sweet and slightly creepy to think of them

making love when we were."

Sarah jabbed me in the side. "They don't do that. Ever."

"How come they didn't announce it?"

Sarah gave me a look that implied *would you after everything*?

"Right. We'll have to celebrate with them when… we can. No other Petries."

Ethan approached Maddie and Gabe. "Congratulations."

Allen bum-rushed his brother, knocking him to the ground. "Congrats, Bro!"

They rolled around on the snow, until Allen let Gabe up, Maddie giving him a hand. Ethan helped Allen up.

The rest of us swarmed Maddie and Gabe, hugging and saying our own congratulations.

Finally, Sarah motioned for all of us to go inside. She had to give Allen the Mom stare to stop him from pelting his brother with the snowball in his hand, reigniting the war. Allen tried to maintain his composure, but Sarah kicked up the look another notch, causing Allen to drop the snowball at his feet.

Ethan laughed, wrapping his arm around Allen and giving him a noogie.

Sarah and I rounded up the kids.

Once inside, Sarah said, "I'm starving."

I glanced at Ethan, and he nodded.

I kissed Sarah's cheek. "I think it's time for me to take Ethan to the airport."

Casey peered up. "Can I come along?"

"Sure. Let's pack some food for the ride, but we need to hurry and hit the road."

Sarah wrapped her arms around my neck. "Drive safely please." She whispered in my ear, "I'll never forgive you if you let me deal with Tie and Peter all on my own."

I laughed. "Next Christmas, no Petries other than us and the children. Promise?"

She put out her pinky. "I swear."

CHAPTER FOURTEEN

Casey and I trooped into the kitchen a little after one.

"How were the roads?" Sarah asked, arranging cold cuts and cheese on a platter for the guests.

"Not bad once we got onto the highway."

Casey snatched some cheddar cheese. "Now, Allen needs my help with the puzzle. We won't be beaten." She headed for the family room.

"It's sweet how close those two are." Sarah smiled. "And I'm glad she feels so at home here, considering the turmoil that must be occurring in her home."

"They're probably at the same mental age. Allen is—"

Sarah flashed her palm. "Stop right there. He reminds me so much of someone I know and love. Who also didn't have the best childhood, in a different way."

"True. I was the forgotten one, and he was the hidden one." I shook my head. "I sincerely hope he finds his Sarah to help him become the person he can be." I wrapped my arms around her waist.

Sarah blinked. "Wow. That… speechless."

I leaned in for a kiss, but was rebuffed with a finger on my lips.

"Aren't you curious about your Christmas gift? The big one?" she asked.

"What?" With all the drama, I hadn't taken notice of the missing gift. She'd always gone out of her way for one. "Does it have to be given in private? Because I have ten minutes right now."

"Just ten?"

"I love it when you get hot and bothered. Will eleven suffice?"

She smacked her lips. "You drive me insane."

"Hopefully in a good way, at least part of the time."

"Why else would I keep you around?"

"I'm good at diaper duty, as I proved yesterday, and I clean Hank's litter box twice a day. Sometimes three."

"Two excellent qualities. You done?" She arched one eyebrow, which connected directly to my hot zone.

"Haven't even started but I think you're talking about something else. So please continue." I waved with my hand for her to go on.

"This spring break, you and I are going to Berlin."

"Shoot." I snapped my fingers. "Last night, I invited Allen to a conference in Boston during his spring break."

"Aw, that's sweet."

"Won't that cause a problem with the trip, though?"

She smiled. "I know about your conference, honey. It's been on the calendar for some time. Your school has a different spring break than CU." She spoke in her patient mom voice so I'd understand what should have been clear in the beginning—she was talking about two different weeks.

"Right. My conference is two weekends after my spring break." I furrowed my brow, seeing another potential flaw in her plan. "Just the two of us?"

"Mom's watching the twins. Airfare is booked. Hotel confirmed. Reservation to visit the Reichstag made."

"The Reichstag—you do know the way to my heart. I can show you all the bullet holes from World War Two. It's a beautiful building, and leaving the scars—it's fitting."

"Yes, exactly what I was hoping for. Bullet holes." She couldn't keep the glee from her eyes, knowing I loved the gift.

This time when I leaned in for a kiss, I was met with hungry lips. "Thank you."

"Merry Christmas, Lizzie."

"I still have eleven free minutes on my schedule," I whispered in her ear.

"I was just going to head upstairs to change into... something else."

"You go first. I'll follow."

* * *

IN OUR WALK-IN CLOSET, I sighed into Sarah's neck, after getting her to come with my fingers.

Her fingers still dug into the flesh on my naked back. "I can't believe we just did that."

"Coming out of the closet is so overrated."

She laughed. "I can't remember the last time we did this."

"Uh, this morning." I still held onto her tightly, as her body continued to tremble.

She bit my neck. "Not sex. Me with my pants around my ankles, you with only a shirt off. The bathroom door locked and the closet door firmly shut."

"I don't think we've ever had sex in here. It's making me think about all the other nooks and crannies we haven't broken in. We do live in a mini-mansion. So many possibilities to be naughty together."

"And you do love a challenge. Do you envision us always

having the guests from hell during these adventures?" Sarah pulled away and yanked up her jeans.

"These people are never allowed in my house again."

Sarah narrowed her eyes. "We'll see about that." She opened the closet door. "I'm going to clean up as much as possible without showering and head downstairs. Hang back here for a few."

"Right. To throw off the masses." I saluted. "And, to take care of things." I waggled my eyebrows seductively.

Her eyes wandered down to my crotch. "No, don't. I want you to explode later."

"You're killing me!"

"I know." She planted a sensuous but much too short kiss on my mouth. "It'll be worth it."

Moments later, I rejoined her in the kitchen, where she'd picked up prepping the lunch trays. "Another meal already?" I consulted my watch. I'd only been gone a little over three hours, and the closet adventure had been brief. "Brunch wasn't that long ago, and it included breakfast and lunch, if I'm understanding the word correctly."

Sarah shrugged. "Not sure what else to do. The conference is still going on in the library. Or maybe they've climbed out the window, which is the option I'm hoping for."

"It would be convenient. Hell, I'd pay for a bulldozer to make an exit for them. What can I do to help?" I pushed up the sleeves on my sweater.

"Start bringing the food out. Let me think." She tapped a nail against her front tooth. "In the dining room, I think." She contemplated the logistics. "Yes, dining room. I'm going to check on…" She left the kitchen before clarifying, but I was certain she meant she wanted to find out where the troublemakers were, and she wasn't referring to Ollie, my favorite pot stirrer, who the last time I saw was with Rose, Demi, and Freddie at the craft table.

Maddie, who hadn't said a word about the Peter powwow since leaving the library, set about dumping a bottle of champagne into a punch bowl and mixed in orange juice and Grand Marnier. I questioned her booze to orange juice ratio, as in not enough booze.

"Must have drinks for round two of brunch. If the Petries are going to have an epic meltdown, I don't want to be sober for it," she said.

"I'm going to rally *all* the troops." I stressed *all*.

Maddie added a few more drops of Grand Marnier. "Okay."

I sidled next to her. "Don't be shy."

"Have I ever been?" She appeared slightly insulted.

"And this is not the day for you to change." I motioned for her to keep going with the liquor.

She looked up. "Wait. You want me to really spice it up?"

I scouted over my shoulder. "Any chance we can knock out a few guests? You failed in your mission last night."

She squinted one eye. "Could be dangerous."

"It's already dangerous, but hey, that's the Petries. And, we need to chill some nice bottles of champagne to celebrate." I squeezed her shoulder.

"Sarah's on it."

Of course, she was.

In the living room, I clapped my hands together. "Okay, folks, lunch is ready."

George rose with a smile, and I wondered how much he perceived what was going on around him. Or maybe living alone after his wife's death made him crave any type of family contact and the poor man was stuck with mine.

Tie, all smiles, looped her arm through George's.

Peter stormed into the dining room, teeth clenched, grabbed a plate, angrily tossed ham and turkey slices onto his plate, and then speared olives with a toothpick until there was a small mound.

Everyone gave him a wide berth.

Even Tie seemed a tad cautious.

Gabe walked into the dining room, dressed in a jacket fit for someone roughing it at the North Pole. Had he been shoveling again? From the angry expression on his face, whatever he'd been up to had put him in a piss-poor mood. He jerked his head, and Maddie trailed him out of the room.

Sarah laser-locked eyes on me.

I sucked in a deep breath.

Peter stalked out of the dining room, and I tailed him to the living room. He took a seat at the fireplace, angling his body to avoid eye contact with anyone, spearing a block of cheddar with a toothpick but not eating it. Just twisting it in the air like a toy.

Dad and Helen, with their plates, huddled near the tree, whispering in each other's ears, occasionally looking in Peter's direction like parents who'd been called to the school to pick up their child after being expelled.

Tie and George sat on one of the couches, George's face aglow as Tie hand-fed him a sweet pickle, Tie whispering, "That's a good boy."

The image and words did my head in, my stomach swirling.

Allen and Casey, stationed at the puzzle table, watched over the kids in the family room, hopefully out of harms way.

Maddie sashayed in, making her way over to Peter, and sat on a chair near him.

Peter scrunched one eye and appraised her face, before returning his dazed look back at his plate.

Neither of them spoke, and I wondered if Peter knew she was now engaged to Gabe. Not that I had any intention of filling in the gap of time since he'd fled to the library.

My wife gave me a trip to Berlin.

His…

Rose and Troy, sitting on the two-seater couch, were the only ones in the room oblivious to the tension. Or too happy about their unannounced engagement to let Petrie drama dampen their spirits. I had to admire them. And maybe that was the way to survive my family. Not let them in.

Gabe approached Dad and Helen, whispering something. Dad arched his brow, and Helen had a look of clarity wash over her face. The trio left for the kitchen.

Sarah, with only a glass of mimosa, had just entered the living room and queried me with a raised eyebrow. I shrugged one shoulder.

If this were a horror film, we were nearing the epic head-to-head. Would the monster prevail? The good guy? Neither? Who was who?

Rose's phone buzzed, and she glanced at the screen, perplexed. A second later, she made her way to the kitchen.

Sarah, sitting on the chair opposite Peter, met my eye once again.

I sighed. Taking a seat on the arm of Sarah's chair, I attempted to eat a slice of cheese, but the mixture in my mouth caused my stomach to roil. "Excuse me," I said.

In the powder room next to the library, I spat the food out into the toilet and then splashed cold water onto my face. Gripping the counter with both palms, I eyed my reflection in the mirror. "This is the worst Christmas ever."

A commotion outside the door forced me to act.

Sarah and Rose each had a twin, and Troy cuddled a sleepy Demi. Allen and Casey followed to the front door, Casey with an unopened puzzle box under her arm.

"Mom's going to take the kids to her house to give them a change of scenery," Sarah explained in her tone that screamed, *Don't ask questions.*

"How can I help?" I said, relieved the children, including my youngest brother who was technically an adult but was still a baby on so many levels, would be safe from whatever was brewing.

"We got this. Can you help Maddie in the kitchen?"

My phone rang. "Uh, it's..." I mouthed, "Ethan."

"You should answer." Sarah gave me a chin-up smile.

"Hold on a sec." I stepped out onto the back deck, stiffening at the burst of cold. "Okay, I'm here."

"I'm on the plane, but I got a text from Lisa's uncle. Her mom isn't expected to make it through the night. I hope... I get there in time."

"I am so sorry, Ethan. Please tell Lisa we're thinking of her."

"I will." He paused. "Don't tell Casey anything. I think Lisa and I should be the ones to tell her. I haven't figure out when and if we'll fly her out for the funeral. I need to see Lisa first."

"Gotcha." What was one more secret?

"The flight attendant is giving me the evil eye. I need to shut down. Thanks again, Lizzie. You saved my bacon."

"I love you, Ethan."

He laughed. "I can't remember you ever saying that. You're the sister I always wanted. Bye."

I took a deep breath of the cold air, simultaneously invigorating and freezing my air passages. "Okay, Lizzie. Sarah probably needs you."

* * *

IN THE KITCHEN, Maddie conferred with Gabe in hushed whispers. Did anyone speak in a normal voice anymore?

"Anyone care to fill me in?" I said.

"Not yet. We're convening a family meeting in the living room." Maddie sipped her drink.

If Maddie needed fortification... I cleared my mind to the

best of my abilities. For the most part, I was an observer, considering I wasn't at the center of this storm.

Would I learn Peter did indeed have another baby on the way?

Or, was Tie lying?

Both, if possible. *How would that work, Lizzie?* Stranger things have happened in this family.

As Sarah breezed into the kitchen, some of the stress in her eyes diminished. She kissed my cheek. "The kids are off. How's Ethan?"

I pulled her into the family room and explained the situation.

Sarah smothered her mouth with a palm but was able to shove the news into the recesses of her mind. With a soul-cleansing sigh, she put on her game face. "You ready?"

I shook my head.

She threaded her fingers through mine. "I got you. Always will."

I boosted our hands to my lips and kissed her fingertips. "When everyone leaves, let's have another Christmas. You. Me. The twins. A fucking do-over."

"Sounds lovely."

Hand in hand, we covered the much-too-short route to the living room, where the Peter-Tie confrontation was about to be convened. Who would be left standing?

* * *

PETER STILL SAT in the chair, not looking at anything or anyone. I'd never seen him so lost. Confused. Sad. He wasn't able to muster any anger, which I took as a really bad sign. He was the Scotch-lady's son after all. But, maybe that fact impaired him in this situation. Confronting reality hadn't been her thing.

Tie sat on the couch, close to her husband, yet she seemed so far away from him and the rest of us. Her cocky grin sliced through me. How did a person like her spring to life? Nature or nurture? A combo? Did it matter?

And, Peter?

I had a pretty good idea the Scotch-lady had helped him along on his path to this day. If she were alive, what thoughts would be going through her mind? More than likely disappointment that her son was being bested by the likes of Tie, not understanding Tie was her doing to a certain extent. Peter was an adult and made decisions leading him to today, but my therapist and I constantly discussed self-destructive patterns, such as my attraction to Meg the alcoholic when I was a young grad student. Even if deep down we understood the dangers of associating with people who reminded us of the ones who hurt us the most, as humans, we still craved the familiar. Like a baby wanting her favorite blanket. And breaking the pattern took courage. Luck. Determination. And love from the positive people around you. I had Ethan. Maddie. The twins. Rose. Gabe and Allen. And, most importantly, Sarah.

I squeezed Sarah's hand, which she reciprocated.

Who did Peter have?

Tie wasn't the type to stand by her partner through better or worse. She preyed during the worst of times.

Dad hadn't exactly been there for us much during our formative years. He was trying now, but could the damage be repaired in Peter's time of need, without damaging Peter's veneer of Mr. Tough Guy?

Helen was motherly, but it was difficult to blunt the knowledge that she'd always been in the shadows, supporting Allen the way I couldn't even contemplate. Getting the best of our father, when he'd barely said two words to me whenever in my presence.

I had meant my words earlier to my father, but it didn't make things any easier. Like him, I was only human.

Maddie's feelings seemed to seesaw from love to resentment for squashing her heart.

For obvious reasons, Gabe kept Peter at a distance, but I think he still felt a stepbrotherly connection.

Allen, who had been sheltered in a different way than Peter and I, was too fragile to understand.

As for me, I still didn't know my brother. Not completely. How would I react to whatever was about to happen?

I scanned the room again, and George either had gone home or was lumped into the kid category, shuffled off to Rose's. Probably for the best. However, now that the children weren't present, his "I like dick" interjections could have made the next hour or so more palatable on some level. Eccentricity had merit.

"Peter," Helen started. "I'm going to be blunt. Tie has made it clear she thinks you have another child on the way. Is that true?"

"No," he muttered into his chest, not sounding convincing.

Helen's pursed lips were in tune with my thoughts.

"Tie, I'm not sure how to say this, but it's difficult to believe anything you say." Helen stared her down.

Tie's smile didn't falter. Nor did she defend herself. I had to give it to her because it was more convincing than Peter's mumbled *no*.

"Son," Dad started. "If you do have a baby on the way or out there already, you have an obligation to care for the child."

"Like you did with Allen?" Peter crossed his arms, but his voice grew stronger. "Where were you when I needed you? Or when Lizzie did?"

This was the time Peter used the name I preferred?

Dad didn't wilt. Not entirely. But Peter's words dented his armor when I scrutinized his eyes.

"Are you telling my husband to set up a secret family?" Tie's voice was free of venom.

"I don't have a secret family. I don't have another woman. I don't have anything." Cocky Peter slowly oozed back into form. "That's not true. I have Demi." He whipped his head in Tie's direction. "If you think you're getting custody, you have another thing coming. I'd rather—"

Helen cleared her throat, stilling Peter's words. Had he been about to threaten Tie's life? Not a good sign at all.

And was Peter contemplating full custody? That surprised me. Had he finally cut the Scotch-lady's apron strings? Or was he realizing what damage could be wrought when a child was raised by someone of the same caliber as our mother?

"Yeah, right." Tie crossed her legs, placing her folded hands strategically on her knees as if readying for a photoshoot. "Judges love mothers. Not fathers."

"You are not a mother. It takes more than giving birth to claim that title. Look at Lizzie. She's an amazing mom."

Flabbergasted, I looked to Sarah. She squeezed my hand.

Tie slowly turned her head to me, fixing me with that grin that would terrify a rattlesnake. "And your brother is a terrible husband."

"You knew what you were getting into, my dear," Peter defended. "We had an agreement from the start."

Her stare dug into me.

Why was I in the middle of their marriage? And, what kind of agreement did they have? Peter could sleep with anyone? While Tie did what exactly?

"Things change, Peter." She turned back to him.

"They do. I have."

She scoffed, "Yeah, right. I have proof you haven't."

"You mean this?" Maddie produced the photo of the redhead, displaying it prominently on the table in front of Tie.

Tie narrowed her eyes.

"Which is exactly like this one." Maddie situated another eight by ten photo of the redhead.

Had Maddie sent Gabe to her apartment to search for this photo? That would explain his sour mood when he'd returned. And, it answered one of my questions. Gabe truly loved Maddie to help Peter out of this jam. It didn't soothe my mind about Maddie's feelings for Gabe and Peter, though.

Peter leaned forward in his seat, comparing both photos.

"You're point, Maddie?" Tie's voice didn't give way.

"This is one of the women Peter had an affair with when we were together." Maddie tapped her finger on the framed picture.

"He's loyal to a certain degree. I don't see how that changes things between us." Tie waved to Peter and back at herself.

"He must also be a magician."

Tie's grin faltered. "I'm sorry?"

"The woman died last year. I remember seeing her photo in the obits—because her"—Maddie jabbed a finger at the photo—"image is seared into my brain."

"She died?" Peter scratched the side of his head. "I didn't know."

He wasn't like my father, then. Dad had stayed with Helen. For well over a decade, closer to two.

And how did Peter not know one of his mistresses was dead? Although, it wasn't like I googled people from my past to ensure they were still breathing. However, I had a feeling the number of people I'd slept with was much smaller than Peter's.

Tie uncrossed her legs. "Nice try, but the photos are different. I've never seen that one." She flicked a finger at the one I assumed came from Maddie's collection.

Maddie stood and removed Tie's photo from the frame with the agility of a designer who handled items like that every day.

Sitting next to Tie on the couch, she held the photos side by side. "They are identical. And, I called the private investigator I worked with. After some threats of a lawsuit, he confessed you forced him to supply these photos. I have no idea how you found out I hired a PI, or what dirt you had on him to get him to play ball..." She shrugged.

"Please. The man would say anything if you give him enough money." Her grin slid into pursed lips.

"You're only proving my point, Tie." Maddie relished exaggerating her name. "And, I happen to know it's impossible for Peter to impregnate anyone."

"That's enough, Maddie," Peter spoke through clenched teeth.

"Are you accusing me of cheating? Suggesting Peter isn't Demi's father?" Tie placed her manicured hand on her chest.

"Oh, no. She has Peter's smile. But, after..." She seemed to mull over the next part carefully. "Getting you pregnant, Peter got clipped."

If that was the case, why didn't Peter own up to that earlier when everyone was silently, or not so silently considering I hadn't been involved in the library talk, thinking Tie's accusation was a foregone conclusion?

Tie studied Maddie's face and then Peter's scrunched brow. "And you know this how?"

"I was with him when he went to the appointment."

"Why in the world would you go with him for that?" Tie's steely veneer started to falter.

"He asked."

What an odd fucking request for my super-uptight brother to make. What'd he say? "Oh, hey, what are you doing Monday? I'm getting neutered like a puppy and would like some company. We can do lunch after."

And he'd asked Maddie, not his wife. Granted, I knew he was still in love with Maddie, but... something niggled at my memory. Peter had slept with Maddie soon after Tie got pregnant. Had he gotten Maddie pregnant that night? Was that why he voluntarily had a vasectomy? Or, did the Allen bombshell spur the decision? He didn't want to end up like Dad, having a secret family? That seemed more likely. Surely Maddie would have told us if she was pregnant.

Did she…?

Was it my business? And how did one ask their best friend, "Hey, did my brother get you pregnant in my home?" The old Lizzie may have asked, but the new Lizzie… who the fuck knew? At the moment, I didn't want any more secrets spilling out into the open.

The room was silent.

I wanted to channel George and blurt out, "I like dick!" to break the tension, but given the topic at hand, it was probably for the best George wasn't here and for me not to mimic him.

* * *

THE FAMILY MEETING came to an uneasy close, with nothing being resolved. Tie, even in the presence of Maddie's evidence, held firm after recovering from the vasectomy news. She clung to her belief that Peter hadn't been clipped and was a father to-be. It was like she couldn't abandon the script in her head. The one she'd planned. That was becoming clearer and clearer.

I wondered if Peter would present his medical records either to her or in court.

Dad pulled Peter aside for another chat. Then Maddie. Finally, Tie. For a while, I fretted I'd be called into his office, my library.

"Maybe we should move," I said to Sarah, helping her load lunch plates into the dishwasher.

She nodded, resting against the counter, her arms crossed. "Any teaching opportunities in the Arctic?"

"I like where you're going with this." I shut the dishwasher, hitting the buttons to start the load. "People are so overrated, especially if related to you."

"Me?" She clutched the front of her sweater. "It's your family causing all these issues."

"I didn't mean *you*, you. Just saying in general." I tugged her arms apart. "I need a hug."

She complied with an embrace conveying she had me, through thick and thin.

"Break it up you two. People might think love exists without a doubt," Maddie teased.

"Says the woman who got engaged hours ago," Sarah retorted, leaning her head against my shoulder as if unwilling to break off all contact.

"Yeah… and then all of this. It's doing my head in," she whispered, scouting over her shoulder after the words escaped.

"Please, Maddie, don't let Peter and Tie influence any life decisions. They are not normal."

I nodded in agreement.

"I'm trying to block everything out today, but…"

"It's way too early for cold feet."

"Well, I went into a tailspin when we got engaged, and it worked out for us," I confessed, wrapping an arm around Sarah's shoulders.

She laughed. "I seem to remember a lot of angst during that tailspin."

"And yet, you're laughing now. So, like I said, it worked out." I waggled my brow at her.

She elbowed my side.

I wanted her.

"What if you two are the exception and not the rule,

though?" Maddie opened the fridge and pulled out a bottle of champagne. "No reason to let this go to waste."

"Are you going to include Gabe?" I asked, still relishing the thought of taking Sarah back upstairs for some alone time.

"Did someone say my name?" Gabe, with his showman smile firmly affixed, strolled into the kitchen.

I had to wonder how confident he was about his engagement considering everything.

Maddie glanced around him. "Good, it's just the four of us. Will you do the honors?" She handed the bottle to Gabe, but I noticed a frostiness to her tone.

Sarah pulled out four flutes, placing them on the island.

He peeled the foil back from the Dom Pérignon, turning away from all of us to pop the cork. The bottle fizzed and Gabe laughed as he quickly poured into one of the glasses, not wanting to waste a drop.

All four filled, we raised the glasses.

"To my brother and my favorite pain in the ass. May you two be as happy as I am with Sarah." I wasn't happy with my speech considering Maddie's sour mood, but I didn't want to be the one to clue in Gabe that all might not be well between the two. If he hadn't noticed, he was a moron.

The doorbell rang.

I jerked my head to Sarah, with a creased brow.

She hefted her shoulders.

I set the flute down on the island and left to answer the door, and there was Matthew, my dad's driver. "Oh, come on in."

"That's okay, ma'am. Is Mr. Petrie here?"

Dad didn't need beckoning. "Matthew, give me one minute."

I stood in the entryway, confused. Were Dad and Helen fleeing the ship? Would they pick up Allen from Rose's? Why couldn't I go? Or was this an old versus new family thing?

Dad returned with Tie on his arm. "Matthew, can you please drive Mrs. Petrie home?"

Matthew dipped his head.

Tie, tight-lipped, didn't speak. Dad had one of her arms in a restraint with his meaty arm. He whispered something in her ear. She paled slightly but did her best to recover. With a nod, she left my home.

When the door closed, I looked him in the eyes. "What? How?"

"I have some experience with women like Tie. I made her an offer she couldn't refuse."

"You bribed her."

He tossed his hands up in the air and then crooked his arm for me. "Shall we see where the rest of this day goes?"

* * *

"Shrimp cocktail?" Maddie, poised with a tray on her right palm, did her best French maid impression, minus the outfit—which was somewhat surprising given the past forty-eight hours and her penchant for flair.

"We just had second brunch," I said.

"So what? Typical isn't a Petrie thing, and food soothes the soul."

Gabe and Peter each selected one, dipping theirs into the cocktail sauce.

"Thanks, Mads," Peter said, still looking pale from earlier events.

Gabe's smile had a hint of a threat. "Yes, thank you, sweetheart."

"Lizzie?" Maddie widened her eyes.

I waved no, adding, "I'm good, thanks."

"Right. Shrimp is too exotic for the likes of you." She sashayed to the other side of the room.

"I just don't want to ruin my appetite for dinner," I muttered to her back.

She waggled her fingers as if saying, "Yeah, yeah."

She made her rounds in the living room, and only Casey, who had returned with Rose and everyone else twenty minutes earlier, and I passed on the shrimp. Sarah, though, was in the kitchen, so maybe she hadn't eaten any.

Gabe's laughter forced me out of my head, and I gathered I'd mentally checked out of the conversation. All I wanted was for everyone to leave. Casually, I consulted my watch to see how long I had disappeared inside my head, a habit of mine when stressed, but I couldn't remember the last time I'd looked at a clock. I'd probably drifted away longer than I'd realized. I waited for an appropriate time to say, "Excuse me. I'm going to see if Sarah needs any help."

Casey tailed me, slipping her hand in mine. "Do you think Daddy is with Mommy yet?"

I peered down at her. "Not yet. His flight has landed, and he's with your uncle. Soon, your parents will be together. Do you miss them?"

She motioned for me to lift her onto the counter. "I don't want them to get divorced."

Sarah, standing in front of the stove, met my eyes.

"I don't either," I said.

"Do you think they will? Can I have some of those onion things?" Casey asked, pointing at the container.

"Of course, sweetie." Sarah scooped out a small handful of fried French's onions, placing them into Casey's palm.

"Thanks. Do you?" Casey directed the question to me.

I hadn't been able to put my finger on why Casey always talked to me so directly about things that Sarah handled better than I did. I sat on the barstool, facing Casey. "I know your mom and dad love each other very much."

She chewed one of the onions, contemplating this. "Do people who love each other ever divorce?"

How would I know? "That's a good question."

"You always say that when you don't know the answer."

I laughed. "Do I?"

"Have you talked to your mom or dad, Casey?" Sarah swooped in.

She shook her head. "They like to think I don't know what's going on."

I laughed again. "You are more perceptive than most adults I know."

"They shouldn't have adopted me." She popped another onion into her mouth, not showing any emotion.

I blinked, and Sarah dropped the large metal stirring spoon into the silver bowl.

"Casey," I started, unsure how to proceed. "That just isn't true. You should never think that."

"They can't afford me. I get that." She lifted a shoulder. "Daddy hides in his office a lot, trying to figure out how to pay for things. I shouldn't have mentioned cancelling Netflix yesterday. That hurt him."

Sarah circled the island and took the seat next to mine to face Casey. "Sweetheart, you are taking on too much. Neither of your parents would want you to think any of these things."

Casey tilted her head. "But I can't stop thinking them when everything is so obvious. I wish Mommy wouldn't talk so much about me having a sibling. I don't need one. I have the twinks and..." She pointed to Sarah's belly as if Sarah were already pregnant. "Even Demi. She's going to be like me."

Baffled, I asked, "How do you mean?"

She shrugged. "Observant. Her eyes never stop."

I hadn't noticed that, but I trusted the little brainiac.

"Tie isn't a good mother," Casey continued. "I'm glad she left."

Maddie entered, setting the tray and empty shrimp bowl onto the counter. "How are things going in here?"

Gabe, hot on her heels, rushed to the kitchen sink and vomited.

That about summed up everything.

"What the?" Maddie, behind him, patted his back. "Are you okay?"

Gabe tossed chunks again. With his head hanging down over the sink basin, he said, "It just hit me. I'm—" He puked again. "Peter's in the downstairs bathroom."

"Peter's vomiting?" Sarah left, not waiting for an answer.

"Everyone," Gabe managed before the next bout.

"Everyone?" Maddie asked. She turned to me. "The shrimp?"

"Who didn't eat it?"

"You, Casey, Sarah, and me."

The thought of seven adults with food poisoning chilled me to the bone.

Where was everyone puking?

"Oh, God. We only have three bathrooms."

Maddie reached into the bottom cabinet where we kept the pots and pans, yanking out one massive pot and two saucepans. "You remember when you made fun of Sarah for buying a pot large enough to cook a lobster?"

"We're landlocked!"

She handed it to me. "It's coming in handy now."

Allen lay on one of the sofas in the living room.

"You okay, little brother?"

He groaned.

"Where are Dad and Helen?"

He pointed upstairs.

"What can I do for you?"

"It hurts."

"What?"

"My stomach." He bolted up and out the front door.

"That's one solution. Can everyone puke in the snow? Would the runoff get rid of the chunks?" I posed to Maddie.

"These saucepans won't hold much." She held them up to emphasize their smallness, aside from the lobster one.

"Whose idea was the shrimp? No one should ever serve seafood in a landlocked state on Christmas."

"Too late for that rule. Would it be rude for us to slip out with the kids and go to Rose's? In reality, what can we do for everyone?"

She made a good point.

There was a crashing sound upstairs.

"Good Lord, what now?" I ran up the stairs.

Troy was in the guest bathroom, the flower arrangement on the toilet had been knocked into the bathtub. "I'm sorry," he said.

"Don't worry about it. Where's Rose?"

"On the bed."

Still gripping the lobster pot, I went to her.

Rose huddled in the fetal position on the bed, looking as if she was on board a tiny boat in the roughest of seas.

"You might want this." I set the pot on the bed next to her. "Do you need anything?"

"Sarah." She lurched up and reached for the pot.

"Righty-O." I scrammed before seeing my mother-in-law hurl, because really, we weren't blood related, and I wouldn't have stayed even if she was my birth mom.

Downstairs, I directed Sarah to her mother.

Maddie and I met in the entryway as I was on my way to check on Allen and Gabe. "Where are you heading?" I asked.

"Charles and Helen. I hear they're in your room."

"My bedroom? The one I share with Sarah?"

"Unless you have a secret bedroom I don't know about, yes."

First my library. Now my bedroom. We hadn't changed the sheets after having sex this morning. And my father and stepmom—*nope, can't go there*. Not when we were at Defcon Four.

"Where's Peter?" I asked.

"Outside with Allen and Gabe."

"Awesome. Can we lock the door on them? I'm officially done with Christmas." I slapped my hands together as if brushing all this off.

"It's an idea. Is there a possibility we'd be charged with murder or some lesser crime if they froze to death?"

"Not if we all stick to the story of *we didn't know they were outside*."

"Not sure the authorities will believe I didn't take part in plotting to kill my ex-fiancé and current." She closed her eyes. "That's weird when I say it aloud, isn't it?"

"This entire family is fucking batshit crazy. This Christmas is making that more than obvious with each passing second." I left her and checked on the men on the back deck, relieved they'd moved there and not the front porch for all the neighbors to see.

The three of them stood in a row, puking on the tallest mound of snow. I think there were Christmas decorations underneath, which would be promptly tossed as soon as the melt occurred.

None of them had jackets on, but their sweaty faces testified they weren't feeling the cold.

"Okay, gents. Tell me what you need?"

"To die," Allen said.

"Not on my watch. At least not on Christmas. Sarah would never forgive me."

Gabe started to laugh, which turned into retching. "The things we do for love."

"I think not killing family members on a major holiday is the goal of most."

"You seem to be failing at the moment," Peter deadpanned.

We all laughed.

Then they vomited.

"I think that's my cue to check on the folks inside. Can I convince any of you to come back in the house? We have a tarp in the garage. I can set you up in the living room."

They waved me away.

Sarah was in the kitchen, gathering cleaning supplies.

Casey was in the family room, watching the cartoon version of *How the Grinch Stole Christmas* with the kiddos. She was a bit young for babysitting, but it was all hands on deck.

"What do I need to do?" I asked.

"Go back in time and knock me in the head when I suggested having everyone over for Christmas."

"If I'd known that was an option, I would have considered. It's like a plague has descended on our house. We may have to burn it down and start all over again."

She stood close. "Did you know your father is in our bed?"

"Please. I've been trying to block out that tidbit since I heard. When was the last time we changed the sheets?"

"What are you two talking about?" Maddie asked.

"Sheets. We need to get sheets on all the couches. Get everyone settled. They can't keep puking, can they?" Sarah answered. "We don't have any Gatorade."

"What? You didn't foresee this turn of events and plan for it?" Maddie mocked. "Who's going to be the bigger baby out of the men? Rose and Helen, who have given birth, will be tough."

"It has a way of toughening up women." Sarah placed a hand on my shoulder. "Thank goodness you didn't have any shrimp. You can be a bit—"

"Please. I'm the toughest."

"Fine. You carry our next child." Sarah crossed her arms.

"But... I work."

She darted her eyes. "That's what I thought. Can you run to... is 7-Eleven still open?" She wheeled around to Maddie, who shrugged. "Hopefully, they are. We'll need lots and lots of Gatorade." She instructed Maddie, "Let's put Gabe and Allen in the library. Peter in the living room. Mom, Troy, Charles, and Helen are settled." She made a chop-chop motion, and we set up the Petrie Christmas triage.

CHAPTER FIFTEEN

"Oh, wow. That was hell." Maddie collapsed on the couch in the family room. "This may go down as the worse Christmas in history."

Sarah nodded. "The good news is it may have cured me of wanting to throw these bashes. Honestly, I don't know if I want to see any of them ever again."

Casey, leaning against Sarah, said, "I had the best job. How much did I earn for babysitting?"

I was about to argue, but Sarah cut me off. "Ten an hour."

Casey quickly said, "Fifty bucks. Awesome."

Christmas was usually an expensive time of year, but this one was racking up quite the fee with the gifts, bribes, and now babysitting fees.

"We'll need you to sit again tomorrow. Everyone is going to be pretty weak after all this."

I groaned. "Really? Can't they go home yet? The roads are clear."

"We'll see. Mom and Troy can probably make it, but I'm not sure I want them on their own. Not after we poisoned them."

The shrimp hadn't been my idea. I only liked it thoroughly

cooked, fried, and doused in some Asian sauce. And even then, I had to be in the mood, which was rare.

"Where are we going to sleep?" Casey yawned.

"Do you want to camp in the nursery? We can set up cushions and blankets." Sarah held her close.

"Can I do that in here? Stay with you guys?" The usually confident Casey morphed into the little girl she was.

"Of course, you can." I hopped off the couch. "Let's steal the cushions from the living room to make you a pillow fortress. We can even steal Uncle Peter's out from under him if he's sound asleep."

"That wouldn't be very nice. He's sick."

"Right. I'll try to refrain."

She cocked her head. "Did you two always hate each other?"

We left Sarah and Maddie in the family room to scavenge.

"That's a—"

"Good question. Got it. You haven't figured out your relationship with Uncle Peter yet."

"I'm not sure that's the case. We didn't have great childhoods. It took a toll on each of us in different ways."

Her little face peered up at mine. "Are any families perfect?"

"No. Perfection is a mirage. Chasing it only wears you out."

Peter slept facing the back of the couch, his breathing deep, his pallor still sickly white.

Casey placed a finger to her lips. She removed one cushion from the vacant sofa, and I grabbed the remaining two.

"We need blankets."

I nodded. Sarah's shopping habit was coming in handy today. The lobster pot. A plethora of sheets and blankets. And God knows what else we'd used since the poisoning. Thank goodness George had left before the shrimp was served.

The four of us built a rather impressive makeshift tent resembling something I imagined Ernest Hemmingway stayed in while hunting kudu in Africa.

Casey clambered under the top sheet with my Kindle Fire and headphones to watch cartoons or probably a documentary that would go over my head. Soon enough, we heard her softly snoring.

Sarah and I snuggled on the leather sofa, and Maddie settled in the chair, her legs pulled up underneath her.

"I have to say, Sarah, as far as holidays go, you went out of your way to make this the most memorable."

I froze on the couch, but Sarah burst into laughter. "Oh, God. Anything and everything that could go wrong did."

"It did," Maddie agreed. "And it didn't."

"What do you mean?" I asked.

"Setting the shrimp poisoning aside"—she pretended to stick a pin in it—"Ethan arrived in the nick of time to be with Lisa on one of the worst days of her life. That has to mean something to her. And it was Lizzie, here, who made sure that happened." Maddie feigned an *I can't believe I said that* expression.

"Poor Lisa. To lose her mom on Christmas." Sarah snuggled further into my arms.

Maddie grew thoughtful for a moment. "Gabe asked me to marry him."

"Does it count when he's holding you hostage?" I asked, wondering if that portended anything.

She laughed. "You've been Sarah's hostage for years."

"From the first moment I stared into her eyes." I kissed the top of Sarah's head.

"Geez, Lizzie. You're making it harder and harder every day to treat you like a moron."

"Oh, sorry. I'll try to fix that. I really don't need the two of you expecting things from me. Ever."

Sarah needled me with her elbow. "It's too late. I figured out your act pretty quickly."

"And you didn't tell me?" I asked.

"It's cute, and I may be a glutton for punishment."

"Hence the desire to plan a Petrie Christmas extravaganza."

"Mark my words; this is the last."

Maddie and I locked eyes. "Can you repeat that?" She whipped out her phone. "I want to record it."

"I'm not that bad."

Both Maddie and I grew eerily quiet.

"Am I that bad?"

I held out a finger and thumb with barely a space between them.

She drilled her elbow further into my gut.

"There's another Petrie situation, and I haven't decided if it's for the best or not." Maddie pressed on.

"Tie," Sarah said.

"Tie," Maddie repeated.

"How can it be bad? She and Peter were miserable. Unfortunately, it means I lost the bet."

Sarah laughed. "I'd forgotten about the divorce bet. What'd we wager?"

I whispered in her ear, fibbing, "You have to sit on my face."

She laughed harder. "Not tonight."

"Ew! No sex talk!" Maddie covered her ears.

I glanced to ensure Casey was still in dreamworld.

Maddie mouthed sorry.

"I fear what Tie is plotting right at this moment." Sarah shivered. "The woman isn't done. Not by a long shot."

"Let's hope Charles and his lawyers are on it. Surely he made a few calls before nearly dying."

"How do you feel about Peter?" Sarah asked.

Maddie started to speak but took an extra tick before saying, "It's weird. There was always a part of me that wondered what he would have been like if he wasn't a Petrie. Not raised to believe cheating was okay. And then there's his dedication to work, another annoying Petrie trait." She glared at me, another workaholic. "But, with Gabe, it's nice—easy even. He can be a little smarmy when it comes to business, but I think that's more an act to cover his insecurity. I don't think he's as insecure as Peter. I think that's the difference."

I had no idea how to respond to this revelation.

"It's funny. Even though this family is insane on all fronts, since meeting the Petries, I've felt like I belonged. Marrying Gabe seems so natural."

"Natural and Petries. Careful, Maddie. Those two don't go together," I said.

"Surely Gabe won't be as insane. He's not a true Petrie after all." Maddie's confident expression wavered some.

"For your sake, I hope he's everything you want from a partner." I boosted Sarah's hand to my mouth. "It makes life so much easier having someone who loves you by your side."

CHAPTER SIXTEEN

Sarah fell against me. "I didn't think we'd pull it off."

"What? Christmas?" I steadied her in my arms.

"Getting them out of the house. Most of them at least."

It was December twenty-seventh, and we'd finally managed to transport Rose, Troy, Helen, Dad, and Allen to Rose's place. They were all still weak from the food poisoning, but I think the group wanted a change of scenery. And Rose had more spare bedrooms. Even Allen had a twin bed instead of a sofa.

Maddie, whose parents had finally arrived the night before, whisked Gabe to Vail. I was willing to wager by early morning, my stepbrother would be on the ski slopes. He always seemed to have a reserve of energy when fun was to be had. Or possibly he didn't eat as many shrimp. And, Gabe had a lot to live for at the moment, while Peter didn't.

The only family members, besides the twins, under our roof were Peter and Demi. Peter was zonked out in the guest bedroom, wearing Gabe's pajamas. I wasn't sure he knew that tidbit. Demi was in a crib in the nursery.

"Everyone's asleep." I brushed Sarah's hair off her forehead and placed a tender kiss above her right eyebrow.

"Dead to the world," she mumbled into my sweater.

"We should get some rest."

Sarah nodded, kissing the side of my neck.

"If you keep that up, we won't actually get any rest."

"And that would be bad because…?" She nibbled on my earlobe before sticking her tongue in my ear.

My knees went weak. "Not bad. Simply pointing out the consequences of you doing this to me."

"If I remember correctly, I owe you from Christmas morning and the rendezvous in the closet."

My arms tightened around her. "I'd completely forgotten."

"I always keep my promises." Her hands were on my belt.

"One of the things I admire about you." I walked backward to the edge of the bed, bringing Sarah with me.

"What else do you admire?"

I laughed. "Fishing for compliments? Really?"

She lowered my jeans just enough and reached into my panties, sliding her finger over my swollen lips. "Refusing me? Really?"

"Wouldn't you prefer a list when I'm not distrac—"

Her finger delved inside me, briefly. After pulling out, she continued to undress me from the waist down. "You were saying?"

"I have absolutely no idea."

"Just because you're adorable, I won't stop." She yanked my top layers off in one motion, leaving only my bra in place. "I like it when you're out of clean bras and have to wear one of mine."

I glanced down at her lacy sugar plum push-up bra. "You like me in this?"

"I do."

"We always buy you sexy things."

She ran a finger down my stomach. "I'm more than willing

to buy you lingerie if you'd wear it. This might happen more." She nibbled on my bottom lip.

"I'd wear a cilice if that meant I'd get laid more."

Sarah's face pulled up, and she peered into my eyes. "A what?"

"You know, a hair shirt."

She laughed, shoving me onto my back and climbing on top of me. "Only you would bring up a garment worn as a form of penance when your wife is getting ready to go down on you." She cupped my cheek. "So fucking adorable."

"Only you think that about me, for which I'm truly blessed."

"Do you often talk to other women like this when being intimate?"

I closed one eye. "Let me think. I talk to a lot of people in my line of work."

Sarah sunk her teeth into my neck. Reaching under me with one hand, she unhooked my bra.

"Not really a punishment." I writhed underneath her.

She raked her nails down my front. "How's this?"

"Fucking fantastic."

Sarah dug her hip into my pussy. "And this?"

"A-mazing."

She kissed me on the lips, hard, her tongue seeking mine.

Even after everything we'd been through over the years, I still craved the simplest of acts with Sarah. Like kissing. Which we continued to do for many minutes all the while her hip ground into me. I wrapped my right leg around her torso.

Sarah's mouth trailed down my chin, past the nape of my neck, landing on my left nipple. Teasing it with gentle licks, she brought it to life, sucking the hardening nub into her mouth. My head sunk into the mattress. Her hands trailed up and down my body, eliciting a tingling expectation in every nerve ending.

She paid my other nipple some attention, biting it harder, causing me to twist even more with anticipation.

She continued her trek downward, peppering my sides and stomach with soft kisses and nips. She dipped her tongue into my belly button. Not staying for long.

Her mouth reached the speckling of pubic hair. "You haven't shaved recently. I like it."

"Glad my laziness has some benefits."

She tasted my clit.

My hips lurched upward.

She moved onto my inner thigh. Licking. Biting. Back to licking.

Lifting my right leg onto her shoulder, she continued paying attention to the fleshy and most sensitive part of the thigh. "I'm loving the view." She waggled her brows as her eyes devoured what I imagined was a glimmering pool of readiness for her.

"Mine's pretty fucking fantastic as well."

"I'm still clothed," Sarah teased.

I tapped my forehead. "I have a very active imagination."

Removing my leg from her, she hoisted her shirt off. "Does this match what you're envisioning?"

"Close. For the top half."

"Are you asking me to strip completely?"

"Do I have to verbalize the request?"

She smiled. "I think I'll let you take them off after..." She left the rest unsaid.

"Deal." I winked at her.

Sarah separated my swollen lips with a finger, not penetrating me quite yet. I wasn't sure she planned to. She loved the challenge of getting me to come with only her mouth. Especially when we had plenty of time to enjoy each other.

Her face lowered closer and closer to my magic spot.

Once again, she tasted me, lapping my juices, slowly and seductively.

A tiny groan escaped me.

Sarah flicked my clit.

I arched my back ever so slightly.

She circled it, applying just the right amount of pressure as it continued to swell. Noticing, she sucked it into her mouth lustfully, before returning to her sensual flicks of her tongue.

My hands reached for the sides of her head, holding her in place. Not that she would pull away now. Sarah loved to tease, but she was never cruel enough to yank me out of the moment entirely.

The closer I got, the more she amped up her efforts.

She slipped a finger inside, quickly adding a second.

My back arched further, and my breathing quickened.

Sarah's attention to my clit intensified as she drove deep inside.

"Oh, Sarah... Don't stop."

She didn't. The opposite exactly, shoving deep inside and pulling her fingers upward, hitting the right spot, spilling me over to bliss.

My entire body trembled.

My legs tightened around her.

My fingers dug into the sides of her head.

"Jesus!" I whispered.

Sarah stilled her tongue and fingers, letting the crest of orgasm rip through my body.

Several spasms later, I pulled her up into my arms. "You're fucking amazing."

"So you tell me. Usually after I get you to come."

"I think it's good to let you know how much I love this. You. Did I mention *this*?" My body quaked again.

She snuggled into my chest. "This is the best way to celebrate the holidays."

"Fucking?"

"Yes."

I started to laugh, but our doorbell rang followed by someone banging a fist on the front door. "What the...?" I conferred with the clock, and it was well after ten at night. "That better not be a Petrie." I leapt out of bed and pulled on a bathrobe. "Stay here."

"No way." Sarah yanked on her sweater.

We bounded down the stairs quickly before the commotion woke the kids and Peter.

When I swung the door open, I spied a police officer and two gentlemen in suits.

"Is Peter Petrie here?"

"Yes," I answered. "He's my brother."

"We have a warrant for his arrest."

"What? Why? How?" My brain spluttered, and all I could think to say was, "He's ill." I added, "Food poisoning."

"May we come in?" asked the younger one in a cheap brown suit.

I stared at him, unsure what to do or say. Was this some sick practical joke of Tie's, or were they really police?

He said, "Please. It'll be easier if you let us in."

"Of course." I waved them in. "Can you tell me what this is about?"

"Where is he, ma'am?" Brown Suit asked.

It seemed useless to try to be cagey considering I already confirmed Peter was in the house. "In the guest bedroom. Right at the top of the stairs."

All three of them charged upstairs.

Sarah wrapped an arm around my shoulders.

Within minutes, the uniformed officer led Peter, still deathly pale and in pajamas and slippers, down the stairs. Upon further inspection, I spied handcuffs on his wrists.

Peter didn't speak, but I said, "I'll call Dad."

"It's freezing out. Can you let him put on a coat?" Sarah asked. "And proper shoes?"

The men relented.

While Sarah gathered the necessary items, I got on the phone with Dad.

The phone rang twice before I heard his gruff hello.

"Dad. It's Lizzie. Peter's just been arrested."

AUTHOR'S NOTE

Thank you for reading *A Woman Loved*. If you enjoyed the novel, please consider leaving a review on Goodreads or Amazon. No matter how long or short, I would very much appreciate your feedback. You can follow me, T. B. Markinson, on Twitter at @IHeartLesfic or email me at tbm@tbmarkinson.com. I would love to know your thoughts.

ABOUT THE AUTHOR

TB Markinson is an American who's recently returned to the US after a seven-year stint in the UK and Ireland. When she isn't writing, she's traveling the world, watching sports on the telly, visiting pubs in New England, or reading. Not necessarily in that order.

Her novels have hit Amazon bestseller lists for lesbian fiction and lesbian romance.

Feel free to visit TB's website (lesbianromancesbytbm.com) to say hello. On the *Lesbians Who Write* weekly podcast, she and Clare Lydon dish about the good, the bad, and the ugly of writing. TB also runs I Heart Lesfic, a place for authors and fans of lesfic to come together to celebrate and chat about lesbian fiction.

Want to learn more about TB. Hop over to her *About* page on her website for the juicy bits. Okay, it won't be all that titillating, but you'll find out more.

Printed in Great Britain
by Amazon